Naomi Serene

Naomi Serene

& The Quest for Knowledge

Piper Sehman

Piper Lee Sehman

This book is dedicated to my wonderful parents. I love you both so much and hope you both know how amazing you both are. Thank you both for everything.

Prologue

Two figures sat across from each other in a dimly lit room.

The man eyed the other immortal cautiously. He could feel the overwhelming power radiating off of them despite being a god himself. If he truly wanted to outsmart the frankly superior immortal, he would most certainly need to be meticulous.

Well, he never was one to back down from a battle of wits, was he? This could be an intriguing challenge.

"Knowledge, I have a proposition for you." His fellow immortal stated in their deep, booming voice.

Knowledge raised a brow, prompting them to elaborate. After observing Creation's stoic expression for a moment, he responded, already able to tell what Creation wanted of him from the glint in their eyes. "You want me to work alongside *her*? What a chore..."

Creation scoffed. "I cannot deny your opinion, but **you** of all immortals should see the *full picture*."

Knowledge paused once more. "I suppose you have a point, but what do you have to gain from this?" Knowledge felt no obligation to offer his services for free, even for the one who technically *made* him.

Creation sighed at the other's ignorance. "Entertainment. After millennia upon millennia of omnipotence, I may finally feel some small sliver of interest."

Knowledge nodded in acknowledgment, perhaps Knowledge could partake in such *entertainment* as well. "One hundred days." He decided "If she cannot even succeed with my assistance in such a time frame, I will not further waste my time."

Creation shrugged. "Very well. Good luck... to both of us."

The immortals stood, returning to their respective sanctuaries.

1

Naomi woke up in a state of shock. It was a rare occasion that she was able to sleep without nightmares and an even rarer one when she woke up after the sun had risen. So, she felt she had a right to be a little confused.

As she lay in bed, her mind slowly began waking up and the memories of what had just happened began to pour into her consciousness. The young woman gasped, bolting upright as her eyes quickly surveyed the space around her.

She wasn't at home.

Instead, she was in an unkempt apartment that must not have been used in a while considering the cobwebs and dust decorating every crevice of the room. But even if the place had been well dusted, it would have still been pretty unpleasant if the smell of burnt carpet and long expired soda was anything to go by.

Naomi stood, her legs aching in protest, but they begrudgingly supported her weight. That was all she needed to get up.

The fuchsia haired girl noticed the room outside of the one she was in had the lights on, so she walked over as silently as possible, old, stained carpet crunching unpleasantly beneath her feet.

When she made her way out into a space that she could only describe as a haphazard fusion of a kitchen and dining room, which also seemed to serve as a makeshift living room, she couldn't contain her shock when she saw two adults quietly having a discussion at the small dining table.

"Mom? Uncle Z?" She gaped.

The talking paused as both adults looked over at her.

Blossom's face broke into a relieved smile. "**Naomi**! I was so worried!" The scarred woman got up and hugged her.

Blossom really didn't look that much different than when Naomi remembered her looking when she herself was little. She had a few new scars, most notably a sizable slash across her nose and a still healing cut through her plump upper lip, but the main difference was that her hair had turned snow white. Naomi dimly recalled Eliza telling her that some forms of harmfully excessive magic could reduce or eradicate melanin production in the body, which was the most likely explanation for the drastic change. It made her look eerily similar to Blossom's own mother.

Naomi was quick to return the hug, gripping her mom like she was a lifeline. "You're... *here*." Even as the words left her lips, she could barely believe them.

Blossom gave her a slight nod and a gentle kiss on the cheek. "Thanks to you."

"Wait..." Panic rose in Naomi's chest as she remembered. "Is Kira alright?! What about Eliza?!"

Z and Blossom shared a quick glance.

"Kira's fine." Z assured his niece. "She's out getting groceries, at the moment. I forgot that we'd need to stock up on food after moving back here." He chuckled sheepishly.

"Eliza..." Blossom pursed her lips. "is awake, but she... doesn't want to be disturbed."

Naomi frowned slightly, confused by the drastic shift in tone. "Isn't that normal for her?" She couldn't help but feel dread rise up in her aching chest despite her feigned nonchalance.

Z sighed worriedly. "Well yes, but-"

A young woman stumbled out of the other bedroom, nervously leaning on the wall as she looked around with an unfocused expression.

Naomi's blood ran cold when she saw Eliza's eyes. They were completely white except for a pale circle of baby blue where her iris used to begin.

Z stood up, quickly walking over to help his daughter. "Need help finding the bathroom, hun?" He asked her softly.

Eliza looked down and nodded, clearly embarrassed.

After Z had led his daughter to the apartment's small bathroom, Blossom spoke again in a hushed tone. "She can't see. Whatever Fate did to her rendered her completely blind."

Naomi felt immensely guilty. She mentally cursed herself for letting Kira and Eliza come with her.

Blossom seemed to notice the shame in her daughter's eyes because she continued. "Eliza doesn't regret coming with you. It was her choice and she wanted to help."

Naomi nodded absentmindedly, pretending to believe her.

Blossom sighed, regretfully moving on. "There's... another thing I should mention." Her voice became a bit detached, almost awkward as she changed the subject.

Naomi sat on the couch to give her legs a rest before turning to face her mother, waiting for her to continue.

"There are two others, the newcomers we found near you three."

Oh, right. Naomi remembered her encounter with Guru. "I know; are you... okay with that?" Naomi inquired cautiously as she remembered what Guru had done to her under Wallo's command.

Blossom pursed her lips. "I am aware *she* wasn't in charge of what happened."

So, that's a no. Naomi mentally summarized. *But she wants to avoid confrontation.*

"The namu, Guru as she called herself, is awake. We've been keeping a watch over her, but Kira insisted that she could handle her today, at least for a while, and..." Blossom sighed. "as much as I hate to say it, you are all adults now... so I convinced Z to let her go out with Guru." Blossom's frown deepened. "But the other... the amourite hasn't awoken..."

"Wait, how long was I out?" Naomi suddenly asked.

"Five days."

"*Five days*?!" Naomi repeated in disbelief.

Blossom shrugged. "Using powerful magic takes quite a bit out of you. Honestly, I was expecting you to sleep for at least a week; that's what happened the first time I..." Blossom trailed off uncomfortably.

Naomi took the hint and let the conversation drop.

Z returned, trying to convince Eliza to stay out in the common area for a bit before retreating to the room she was staying in, which made Naomi think. "Where exactly is Life staying then?"

Eliza jumped. "Oh, Naomi." Z had to turn her head slightly, so she wasn't looking over Naomi's shoulder.

The taller cousin bit her lip. "Sorry for startling you."

Eliza waved her off. "Nothing to worry about. The other girl, I'd hardly call her *Life* now, is staying in the bedroom with me since I'm the quietest. You've been sharing with Kira and her escort."

Naomi rolled her eyes. "I don't think Kira would appreciate you calling Guru an 'escort'." Naomi tried to use the comment to ignore the guilt she felt about taking the only bed in the room. Now that she thought about it, she had seen an air mattress on the floor. That must have been where Kira and Guru slept.

Eliza smirked, seemingly trying to hide some emotions of her own. "I do what I want."

"I've got one last question for now." Naomi decided. "Where exactly are we?"

2

Fate hated this. She hated herself for letting this happen.

How had Blue broken away from her influence? Did it have to do with the Seven of Spades attacking him? Was it a matter of demonic heritage or the something to do with the interference of The Jack of Diamonds?

She shook her head. That didn't matter. What really mattered was how the mortals were able to completely disrupt her plans, even if they were prophecy members, their success was inconceivable.

"Clearly, their success wasn't truly inconceivable, given how they did indeed **succeed**." A cold, deep voice said from behind her.

How did they know what she had been pondering?

Fate froze, angered but perplexed. "Who are you? This is **my** refuge." She could tell they were immortal by their noticeable aura of power. The infringement upon her domain angered her.

"Not anymore. You broke the rules, after all." Fate heard their dress shoes clacking against the solid floor as they drew closer.

Fate decided to turn and face the intruder. Her eyes widened when she instantly recognized his face, even if it was considerably older and more stoic.

Before her was a tall, slender man in an ink black suit and a matching tie. He had pale, almost colorless skin and shoulder length, wavy, jet black hair tied back into a neat, low ponytail. His almond shaped, stark gold eyes glinted mysteriously, as if he had a secret he was purposely keeping from everyone for his own gain. In short, he was absolutely gorgeous.

But that wasn't what was important right then. "Who are you?" Fate repeated firmly.

The immortal extended his hand. "Your new business partner."

3

"This is my old place. I lived here with... North..." Z sighed sadly at the memory of his late brother, "before we moved into the cabin, but after fleeing from the nuclear fallout of our old home."

Naomi pursed her lips, trying her best to ignore the mention of her deceased father, and the depressing image of the bomb that had killed his parents and unborn sister.

"Z and I thought it'd be best if we hid here for a while." Blossom cut in, not wanting to be absorbed by her own grief. "Fate can detect Essence, but if we hide in an area of highly concentrated Essence, she might not be able to find us, or at the very least, it will make the search much more difficult."

Naomi nodded, satisfied with the answer she was given, but before she could stand up and exit the awkward atmosphere that had been created, the front door to the apartment burst open, revealing an ecstatic looking Kira. "We're *baaaaack*!" The brunette declared loudly. Something about her seemed... different, but Naomi couldn't tell what exactly.

Eliza groaned, massaging her temples. "Kira, I don't have the energy to deal with your noise right now. Shut up."

Guru frowned, opening her mouth to say something, but instead, just sighed in a show of relenting. Underneath the baggy T-shirt she was wearing, Naomi saw a hint of her raw, still scarring skin from where The Stone of Evil had been pulled from her collarbone. Naomi grimaced to herself, but tried to look past the area entirely, instead focusing on the excited glint in Kira's eyes.

Kira pretended to ignore her sister. "And you guys won't **believe** what Guru just did!" Guru's freckled cheeks reddened in embarrassment at the apparent reminder.

Z and Blossom's faces grew concerned despite Kira's wide grin. They clearly hadn't grown to trust the blonde much in the last few days.

"She totally **annihilated** my ex!" Kira declared as she set the groceries next to the fridge. "It was insane!"

"She-**he**," she quickly corrected herself after seeing Kira pointedly glance at her. "was making inappropriate remarks towards you. I did what any sensible person would, or at the very least *should*, do." Guru tried to defend herself.

Z's expression became unreadable as he slowly made his way towards Guru. The freckled blonde gulped nervously as the dark haired man approached her.

"You... defended my daughter?" Z asked her quietly.

"I can protect myself!" Kira scowled before looking away bashfully. "But... yeah, she did."

"I tried to anyways. I-I don't think I actually-**O-OH**!" Guru squeaked out in surprise as Z ruffled her hair affectionately, smiling at her.

Blossom stared at the interaction analytically. Naomi couldn't tell what was going through her head.

Kira grinned up at her dad, clearly pleased with how things played out, but soon after admiring the scene, Kira looked over at Naomi, her smile fading slightly. "Hey... can we talk for a minute?"

Naomi raised a brow at the sudden change in tone, but she nodded, getting up and following Kira to their room.

4 |

Several minutes had passed by without Kira or Naomi saying any-thing, so Naomi decided to try and break the silence.

"So-" Naomi cut herself off after noticing something.

She looked at her cousin in surprise. "wait a second... did you cut your hair?" *That* was what seemed so new about her, Naomi realized with a start.

For as long as Naomi could remember, Kira had matched her hair to her mother's in length and style the woman herself had assumed at that age, but now her hair didn't even reach her shoulders, and it seemed a lot messier and much more fluffy with soft curls on the longer bits, perhaps similar to what Z's would look like if he took a bit more care in washing his hair with something other than three-in-one soap.

Kira smiled softly. "Yeah... I've wanted to for a while now, but I was always worried about what Mom and Dad would think. It's a bit more androgynous then they're accustomed to; even when Dad had a pony-tail in his teen years, it was never very *girly*." Naomi tried not to cringe at Kira's reference to her mother as still being in the present.

She didn't remember Kira ever seriously mentioning that she wanted shorter hair. Had she forgotten Kira telling her, or did Kira never say anything to her? Either way seemed strange given how Kira told her basically everything, and Naomi had a pretty good memory.

"What made you change your mind?" She settled on asking.

Kira shrugged, a bittersweet expression painting her face. "I just realized that as hard as I try, I'm never going to be exactly like either of them, so I decided to be more... **me**, I guess."

A few more beats of silence passed by.

In the stretch of quiet, Naomi came to a rather unpleasant realization: She and Kira had been close, even before Naomi and Blue moved in with their uncle and aunt, but Kira had always been the one pushing their friendship along, telling Naomi little things about herself, until those little things became big things, and those big things became secrets. But that never seemed to be the case for Naomi, not after what happened to her parents, she didn't tell anyone her secrets, not even Kira. She'd tell Kira something little every now and then, but she did so in a calculated manner.

"Kira... I think I'm a bad friend..." Naomi said slowly, making Kira look at her in confusion.

Kira's pierced lips curled into a frown. "What d'you mean?"

"I... haven't been telling you things... **anything**, really."

"I know."

"And I-" Naomi stopped herself, quickly replaying in her mind what Kira just said. "You know?"

Kira smiled sadly. "I had a hunch for a while, but it really hit me when this whole *debacle* happened." Kira was quick to continue before Naomi could cut in. "And I know we talked about it a bit back *there*, but we never really resolved things between us. I know my frustration must be matched by some from you, but I've been thinking about it a lot over the past few days. That's specifically why I wanted to talk."

"I want to, Kir, really, but... I don't know how..." Naomi shamefully admitted, not even trying to deny the claim about her own frustrations.

Kira nodded. "I don't have a full plan of how to fix what happened between us, but I have an idea of where we could start."

Naomi raised a brow, intrigued. "I'm listening."

Kira took a deep breath. "I think it's time I let go of my biggest secret... but I don't want to do it alone."

Naomi straightened. "Kira... are you saying what I think you're saying?"

Kira nodded shakily. "I... I think It's time I came out to our family."

Naomi was bored.

She leaned over the side of her bed, eyeing Blue hopefully, but her brother didn't bother acknowledging her. He was far too immersed in whatever he was reading.

The ten-year-old huffed in frustration, kicking her legs impatiently in the air to try and get her twin's attention. When her attempts proved pointless, she couldn't help but feel slightly hurt. Did he really not want to interact with her that much?

But just as Naomi was thinking of leaving her room, there was a knock at the door. She turned to identify her visitor and perked up as her oldest cousin walked into the room.

"Kir!" Her grin faltered when she saw how anxious her best friend looked. "Are you-"

"Can we talk?" Kira quickly asked, playing nervously with her newly pierced ears. "It's... **really** important."

"Sure..." Naomi hopped off her bed, hopefully glancing at Blue and sighing sadly when he didn't even bother looking up from his book. Another painful twinge in her chest to add to her memory, it seemed.

Kira led her out of the room and into the corner of the backyard where they both sat on the grass.

"So... what's going on?" Naomi asked, looking at her cousin curiously.

Kira gulped. "I've uh... been thinking..." Kira bit her lip, shifting nervously. "about... *me*, I guess?"

Naomi frowned in confusion. "Okay... what are you talking about?" Kira wasn't typically so apprehensive about anything. Her cousin was more often the punch first, ask questions later type.

Kira anxiously continued. "What I mean is that I know what I'm thinking 'bout, I just don't know how to *say* it."

Naomi hummed understandingly, so Kira began. "Naomi, do you know what being 'gay' is?" The brunette carded her hands nervously through her long ponytail.

Naomi thought for a moment. "Yeah... I think. Isn't gay another word for happy? Like in Christmas carols and stuff?"

Kira shrugged. "I mean sure, but that's the other meaning of the word. But that's not what I meant."

"Then what *do* you mean?"

Kira took a deep breath before continuing. "It means... you like girls, or guys, if you're a guy."

Naomi blinked. "So... **you** like girls?"

"Yeah..." Kira nodded hesitantly.

"... That's an option?" Naomi wondered aloud.

Kira nodded slowly. "Why wouldn't it be?"

"Oh!" Naomi sighed in relief. "I thought you were gonna tell me you burned down another abandoned building or something!"

Kira cocked her head questioningly to the side. "You're not... weirded out or anything?"

Naomi shrugged. "Why would I be? It's not like this changes you as a person or anything. I don't see anything weird about liking pretty girls."

A large smile spread across Kira's face as the tension drained from her posture. "I'm happy I told you."

Naomi returned the expression. "Me too. Now let's go do something! Blue's busy reading and I'm *dying* of boredom!"

Kira giggled, tugging her out the front door. "Sure! I've got something in mind!"

Dinner that night was surprisingly normal. Naomi guessed that Z and Blossom were trying to maintain as lighthearted and nostalgic of an atmosphere as possible, which she greatly appreciated given everything that happened as of late, even if it felt artificial.

The strangest deviations from normal were Guru's soft spoken responses and occasional little laughs at Kira's jokes, but a close second was the nature of Kira and Eliza's arguments. Of course the pair still disagreed with each other, but it seemed much more playful, and their jabs at each other weren't as mean spirited and ill intended.

After dinner, Blossom rose from her seat, most likely to leave, but Naomi was quick to intervene. "Actually Mom... Kir and I were hoping we could do something as a family after dinner."

Blossom rose a brow, a small smile gracing her pinkish lips. "Oh? Of course, dear. That sounds quite nice."

Z nodded, getting up to help Eliza make her way to the couch. "That sounds like a great idea!" The brunet agreed enthusiastically.

Guru blinked, surprised, but silent as she sat on the floor next to the couch in preparation for whatever activity Naomi and Kira had in store.

"But uh... before that... can I say something real quick?" Kira asked, sweat beading on her forehead.

Z's expression changed to mirror the seriousness he heard in his daughter's voice. "Of course, honey. We're all listening..."

Kira took a deep breath.

Naomi gave her a thumbs up before sitting down and giving Kira the spotlight.

"Well... you all matter a lot to me... and I'm gonna be honest now with you all, so, here goes nothing..." she sighed nervously one more time before continuing, "I... I like girls." Kira instinctively winced, shrinking in on herself.

"... Oh! I thought that everyone fancied women at some point in time!" Blossom exclaimed, more so to herself than anyone else. "We *are* dubbed the fairer sex, after all!"

Naomi's eyes widened at her mother's unintentional reveal. "Wait-"

"Were we supposed to be surprised?" Eliza asked sarcastically. "Kira, you're about as straight as a damn circle." Luckily, Kira seemed to sense the acceptance in her words.

"Did... everyone else have an idea of this beforehand?" Z frowned, surprised, but not upset.

"Yeah."

"Pretty much."

"Well... yes."

"Oh. Well," Z shrugged, getting up to hug his daughter. "I'm glad you told us! Even if I was the only one who didn't know in the end!"

Kira sighed, returning her dad's hug. "Thanks, Dad."

Z rose a brow questioningly. "For?"

"Accepting me."

"You don't need to thank me for that, hun." Z beamed. "I'll love you no matter what."

Enjay woke up with a sharp gasp, feeling surging into her body before she could process what was happening.

Hadn't she found The Book? Why was she still... *herself*?

"Oh. So much for having a silent roommate now." A disappointed sigh followed the disappointed statement.

Enjay's head snapped up, her onslaught of forming questions screeching unceremoniously to a halt in her mind, looking at a girl sitting on a bed and... the blonde wasn't sure what she was doing, actually. She was pulling small devices out of her ears, but Enjay had absolutely no clue what they were. The strange thing is that the blue haired girl wasn't looking straight at her, her gaze was slightly off, pointed somewhere over Enjay's shoulder even though all that was behind her was a wall.

"What... how-"

"You're on an air mattress on the floor of my room."

A mattress made of air? How does that work? The mattress doesn't ***feel*** *made of air...* Enjay was quick to shake the thought away. She had more important things to focus on.

"And you're speaking English thanks to the magic of yours truly." She jabbed a blunt thumb at her own chest. "I was able to transfer some basic information of the language to you. Anything else you *need* to know?" The blue haired girl asked impatiently, clearly wanting to go back to whatever she was doing beforehand.

Enjay blinked, realizing that she was indeed speaking a language she didn't recognize. "Why am I here?" She decided on inquiring. "And... where exactly is 'here'?"

"Well, this is planet Earth. You're in an ex-country called the United States, in a town called Sunny Hills, in a former state called Washington. As for *why* you're here..." The plus sized girl shrugged. "I don't really know, actually."

"You... *don't know*?" Enjay repeated skeptically. "How do you not-"

"I mean, I know that Naomi found you and all, but other than that, I'm not entirely sure on the specifics or the *why*." Enjay huffed indignantly as she was cut off, but before she could do anything about it, a new figure entered the room.

"I heard my name; was I summoned?" A tall girl with deep pink hair peeked her head into the open doorway.

"Naomi Serene, have you been *eavesdropping*?" The blue haired girl accused the taller dramatically.

"Depends on your definition of eavesdropping." The prettier one smirked rather mischievously. Enjay thought the expression suited her well.

The blue haired one scoffed to herself and rolled her eyes. "Kira's really rubbing off on you again, huh?" She grumbled to herself.

Enjay inhaled sharply as she realized something while looking at the attractive, young woman before her and her... friend. "What class are you two?"

"Huh?" 'Naomi' frowned confusedly.

"Beats me." The blue haired girl nonchalantly responded with a yawn.

Enjay blinked in utter disbelief. "How do you **not** know what class you are in?" She asked in disbelief. "For the blue one, I can believe it; there's no way she's amourite, her facial features are too plain."

"Gee thanks." The pale one scowled, but otherwise looked relatively unbothered.

"But for you..." Enjay motioned to Naomi because, in her mind, that explained everything. "High cheekbones, almond shaped eyes with long and dark lashes, you definitely have amourite genes in you."

"Oh uh..." Naomi scratched the back of her neck bashfully. "thank you... I guess? But I think you've got the wrong person, I don't have a set 'class' or anything like that."

Enjay frowned. "No, I'm not wrong. You're likely just a hybrid of some sort, then." She theorized decisively.

Naomi shrugged. "Think what you want, I s'pose. I can take it from here, Liza. You can turn your music back on."

Is she unbothered by such a poignant disagreement? Enjay thought in disbelief.

"It's an *audio book*, actually." The shorter girl corrected haughtily as she reinserted the small devices into her ears.

Naomi snickered. "We should leave, Eliza gets cranky when she's awake this late."

The blue haired girl sent Naomi a glare, even if she wasn't looking straight at her, it was clear who she was directing her expression towards. "I'm **blind**, not deaf. I can still hear you."

Naomi gave her a playful grin. "Yeah, that was the point."

She directed Enjay out of the apartment and into the hallway showing the front doors of other apartments. When they made it outside, Naomi's playful expression immediately vanished, making her look tired. Her aura almost deflated, leaving her looking melancholy and unsure. "Sorry about that... I've been trying to act normal for her; she isn't taking the loss of her sight too well, she's just good at hiding it. But... I probably shouldn't have said anything. Do me a favor and forget what I just dumped on you. Sorry, I don't usually do that."

Enjay couldn't help but feel like Naomi was hiding something too, but she had more pressing concerns to focus on. "I don't understand... why am I not immortal? I read from The Book... I think... I can't entirely remember. Are you a prophecy member? Why-"

"I don't know everything." Naomi started. "But I can tell you that you **were** immortal, you just... switched back."

Enjay frowned. She wasn't an expert on any of this, but she knew immortality didn't work like that. "***How?***"

Naomi pursed her lips, her expression darkening. "If I had to guess... it had something to do with my brother reading The Book, but I can't be sure."

"Your **brother**?"

Naomi's expression grew pained. "Yeah... my brother..."

After a good half a minute of silence, Enjay concluded that Naomi had no intention to elaborate. "You didn't answer my other question... are you a prophecy member?"

Naomi's frown deepened. "I... think so? My parents were, but I'm not sure if-"

"Oh, you definitely are, Miss Naomi."

Naomi's eyes widened. "Shouldn't you be sleeping?" The toned, young woman asked the newcomer skeptically.

Enjay noticed a short girl with pinkish blond hair and rosy, freckled skin emerging from another room. She was cute, Enjay supposed, but nothing special. Not amourite, but perhaps namu or another moderately attractive species. "Perhaps I should be; I would ask the same of you if I was more bold. It doesn't matter, anyhow. Anyone who interacts with an immortal is part of a prophecy. That is a universal rule."

"Oh." Naomi grimaced. "Then I guess I am."

"She is too." The blonde nodded at Enjay. "Everyone currently residing in this apartment is. Mistress- er... Fate had me memorize the Prophecy Decks each time I was reset, so I'm aware who is involved with the current era's prophecies. But even if I wasn't, my intuition would have told me with certainty that you are; it's impossible to be immortal and not be a prophecy member."

A smile crept across Enjay's face. *I guess I became important after all.*

But her happiness was quickly replaced with dread. *But that means...*

"M-my parents..." Emptiness filled Enjay's chest, making her feel alone... and isolated.

Naomi seemed to immediately understand. She looked down and didn't say anything, most likely out of respect since she didn't know anything about Enjay's life.

"M-Fate has been immortal for a little over three millennia." Guru supplied quietly. "And you were already immortal before that... I'm sorry..."

Enjay let out a shaky breath. "I had a plan... I was going to become immortal and wish for their lives to be better... but I never really thought of what would happen *after* my time as an immortal was done. I guess I just assumed I'd be immortal forever. I should have at least given them a proper goodbye... now I don't even get to do that." Words spilled out of her mouth as she looked down at her hands doubtfully. *This isn't what I wanted. Did I... fail?*

"I didn't get to say goodbye to my dad." Naomi said after a while.

Enjay blinked, her lips parting slightly.

"Fate just took him from me... I didn't even know for certain that he was dead until recently." She continued quietly, so that only Enjay could hear.

Enjay's gaze traveled down, fixing on Naomi's scarred arm that she had begun stroking absentmindedly when she mentioned Fate. "Is *that* from this 'Fate' you mentioned?"

Naomi let go of her arm, looking caught off guard. "Yeah..." she didn't elaborate.

Guru backed a few feet away from the other two. "We shouldn't continue this conversation... the Ace and older Jack are returning. I have a feeling they wouldn't like this discussion."

Naomi frowned, her eyebrows knitting together. "And you know that how?"

Guru shifted uncomfortably. "My magic... I can sense the presence of others via their Essence and objects around me with a fair amount of accuracy, but I cannot do much else... it's rather useless most of the time, but in situations like these, it's convenient."

Nami blinked, her expression relaxing. "Oh..."

Why does she seem so suspicious of the freckled one? Enjay couldn't help but wonder. *I guess I'll have to find out somehow.*

Fate didn't exactly remember what happened or how it occurred.

She had never felt such a strong pull of attraction before, and Knowledge seemed to be fully aware of her feelings. He must have had his own, given how many times he kissed and lovingly caressed her.

He was intelligent... as one would expect from the embodiment of knowledge. He was able to help Fate see that there was no need to make a weapon to slay immortals when the object of her hatred was gone. She needed a more relevant goal.

He had a plan that Fate couldn't believe she had never thought of and she was more than excited to put **their** plan into motion.

Mere months had passed and they were already almost ready.

"I can't live like this anymore!" Enjay sneered at the burnt piece of bread in her grasp. "We can't even eat half the time, much less have a decent life!"

"Darling, **please**." A tall woman with long, violet, almost black hair and indigo eyes reached across the table to gently rub the back of her daughter's hand. "All we need is each other. Everything else is secondary." The blonde man sitting next to her silently nodded in agreement.

Enjay glared at her parents. "You say that even after they tried to **kill** you both after your marriage?! After they *ripped out* Dad's tongue for-"

"We can make it through the hard times, Enjay." The dark haired woman said firmly. "We have before and we will again. There's no need to bring sensitive details into your complaints." She carefully eyed her mute husband, who was blankly looking down at his lap, clearly reliving something awful after what Enjay reminded him of.

"*Complaints*?!" Enjay repeated incredulously, standing up from the table in her anger. "This is **my** life! I never asked for this!"

Before her mother could respond, Enjay shook her head firmly. "I want more than this." She snarled, her teeth grit together. And with that, the blonde stormed out of the house, ignoring her mother's calls for her to come back.

Enjay Ellis never ended up coming back after that night.

"So... what's the plan now?" Naomi asked her mom and uncle curiously.

"I... don't think there is one." Z replied hesitantly.

His tone made Naomi suspicious. *He never speaks so carefully unless he's hiding something...*

"What about Blue?"

Blossom and Z shared a glance.

"Naomi... there isn't a way for a mortal to change an immortal back to their previous state." Blossom revealed sadly. "There's nothing we can do."

Naomi tried to hold in her utter disbelief. "But Enjay-"

"We've been over this. Blue mot likely used his wish to free her and the namu as an act of goodwill." Blossom cut her off, clearly not wanting to think about her lost son more than absolutely necessary. "And I'm **not** letting my family grow any smaller."

"If I may..." Guru cut in hesitantly, still wanting to tread carefully around Blossom given the woman's less than pleasant memories of her. "there may be a way we could consider... it's theoretical and dangerous, of course, but-"

"**No.**" Blossom said firmly.

"I think your mom is right, Naomi." Z replied slowly. "I don't think anything we do will help..." He looked away, most likely remembering what happened to his late wife when she tried to intervene. "and it's not worth the risk."

Naomi couldn't help but feel angered by her mom and uncle's lack of consideration. "Do you not care about him, then? *Your own son?*" She hissed at her mother.

"**Naomi Serene!**" Z yelled back at her.

Blossom didn't respond, simply glaring at her lap, frustrated tears shining in her eye.

"Naomi, let's go outside for a bit..." Kira suggested gingerly. "let's get some fresh air, yeah?"

Naomi stood up, marching over to the apartment's front door. "**Fine**. Let's just get out of here, Kira."

Her cousin nodded quickly and jumped up to follow her.

"... What just happened?" Enjay blinked, sitting cluelessly in the now vacated apartment.

"Miss Naomi has a bit of a temper when it comes to situations she invests emotion in." Guru supplied. "Mister Vaden and Missus Blossom are frustrated at her ambition, finding it unrealistic and dangerous."

"In other words, Naomi has a hero complex and it frustrates everyone." Eliza deadpanned.

Enjay pursed her pink lips. "Oh... where do you two stand?"

"I owe Mister Ex-Vaden my life, so I'd gladly attempt to save him, even if it cost me greatly." Guru replied almost immediately. "I'll prove that I can be useful to them..." she said quietly under her breath. Enjay cringed at the determination in the short woman's words, but it'd be hypocritical of her to deny the sentiment.

"I'm not as set in stone as her." Eliza answered with a shrug. "I guess I'm closer to Dad and Aunt Blossom's stance, though; I've never been the biggest fan of Blue."

Enjay frowned at that. "Wait, why don't-**didn't** you like him? Isn't he your cousin?"

Stormy blue eyes rolled in her general direction. "Just 'cuz he's family doesn't mean I have to *like* him." Eliza sighed tiredly. "He's one of those guys that thinks he can solve everyone's problems and thinks we all are just too smooth upstairs to understand what he's really doing. Besides, he never bothered to spend time with any of us, so I gave him the same treatment."

Enjay bit her lip nervously. Why was she nervous? She had only known these people for a short while, and their problems were not her own. They didn't owe her anything. "So are you two going to go with Naomi if she decides to go after him?" The blonde questioned.

"Ah, I suppose..." Guru said, sounding surprisingly hesitant considering her answer a few seconds before. "I don't want to leave Miss Kira so suddenly after we've... gotten acquainted."

Eliza huffed out a laugh at the namu's apprehension. "And Naomi said you **weren't** Kira's escort."

Guru's head tilted as she gave Eliza an innocently confused look. "What's an *escort*? I do not believe the vocabulary you provided me with included that word in whatever fashion you seem to be using it in."

"It's like a prostitute." Enjay answered smoothly.

Guru's face went red in embarrassment. "I-I **beg your pardon**?!" She spluttered indignantly.

Enjay shrugged easily, raising an eyebrow at the reaction. Why was the timid one reluctant to embrace her appeal? Enjay could admit that she had the assets despite not being very attracted to her, so why not take pride in them? "There's no shame in it. If anything, it should tell you that you're attractive. You know-"

"**Alright**, I don't like where this conversation is going." Eliza announced, standing up and slowly making her way to the nearest wall. "I'm out. Don't call me unless there's a fire or something." She declared, feeling her way to the other side of the apartment where her room was.

Guru hummed thoughtfully, her cheeks still heavily colored, showing she hadn't completely recovered from Enjay's remarks. "P-perhaps my magic could prove useful to Miss Eliza."

Enjay raised a brow. "Oh? In what way?"

"Since she cannot see, being able to detect objects near her may help her navigate more efficiently. I suppose I'll ask her for her thoughts on the consideration tomorrow, after she's ready to talk again."

Enjay nodded. "Yeah, Naomi did say that Eliza was bothered by her blindness, so maybe that'll help her."

Guru grimaced. "You... probably should not say such things aloud."

"Why not?" Enjay saw no use in hiding what she knew.

"Miss Naomi seems to be the type to withhold such information to keep it from circulating. If it were my choice, I'd do my best to respect that." The way Guru said her piece was in a very non confrontational manner, making Enjay realize that Guru was giving her a recommendation rather than a critique.

"Oh okay, I'll keep that in mind." Enjay took the information how it was presented to her, a suggestion.

Guru's eyes widened slightly, like she wasn't used to people taking her advice into consideration, but despite that she nodded and hesitantly smiled before standing up to go after Kira and Naomi.

"So basically, your magic would be like a walking stick, except my hands could be free..." Eliza pondered out loud. "yeah, that would be pretty useful. Can you teach me?" The blue haired girl asked, her expression suddenly changing to show her eagerness to learn.

Guru, however, looked pensive. "The only issue is that my magic is self taught. I don't know how to show you verbally because my magic is more of a feeling. I... would require your assistance."

The blue haired girl cringed. "Guru, don't say what I think you're about to say."

Guru bowed her head apologetically, but continued anyway. "W-would it be possible for you to enact another Essence induced exchange of information between us?"

Eliza's frown deepened. "The more I transfer, the less control I have over what I exchange. I don't know about you, but I don't want to share everything about myself just so you can teach me magic."

The former servant frowned in confusion. "But when you taught Miss Enjay English, nothing-"

"Oh, I learned things." Eliza's expression darkened. "I saw things that made me wanna **bleach my eyes out**, even though all I can see now are memories."

Kira rolled her eyes. "Oh come on, Liz, it couldn't be *that* bad."

Eliza immediately caught on to the implied challenge. "You know how she escaped her home planet and began a new life, Kira? She sold *herself* for a ticket on an intergalactic cruise ship. I had to see all that."

"M-maybe you shouldn't reveal such things without her permission." Guru suggested timidly. "But I understand, I-I'll simply try teaching you my magic personally... but be warned, words were never meant to be the form that this magic was taught in... it will be quite difficult for both of us."

"That's a price I'm willing to pay." Eliza decided. "When can we start?"

Guru's shoulders sagged in relief. "How about now?"

Fate stared at the vast amount of smoldering ruins before her.

She had done this. She **wanted** this, and knowing that made her sick to her stomach. How could she bring herself to do something so ravenous? Did she really have so little control over her anger?

She was still fairly certain that she didn't regret her actions, but if that was true, why was there a voice in her head telling her that she should?

She felt a presence behind her. It wasn't a mortal... they were all dead by then. She had made sure of that.

Fate turned, her gold eyes locking with another set of the exact same color.

The slightly shorter goddess had long flowing hair and an outfit embellished with gold and jewels. She looked much more conventionally goddess-like than Fate, who, up until then, had been solely focused on her revenge, and had yet to truly examine her new appearance. She hadn't even bothered with her appearance.

"I did this..." Fate admitted in a whisper. The words felt foreign coming from her, like she still hadn't fully processed what she had done.

The other immortal simply shrugged. "Well, you can't do anything about that now, can you?"

That made her anger flare up with renewed intensity. "How can you be so calm right now?! I just killed an entire **planet** like it was nothing!" Fate demanded.

Again, the other just shrugged. "We're immortals. We have our powers for a reason; we **earned** them. We shouldn't be ashamed of using them."

Fate let the other immortal's words sink in.

I DID earn this.

*I **wanted** this.*

I can't let anything stop me now that I have the power to carry the burden of bringing justice to the universe.

Fate's hands tightened into fists. "What should I call you?"

The blonde perked up. "Call me Lady Life." She curtsied elegantly.

"And from now on, I'm Fate, The Reaper of Justice."

14

Guru was unable to start teaching Eliza immediately like she'd originally suggested.

Blossom sensed Guru's magic activating almost instantly, which made her increasingly suspicious of the blonde. She decided to have Naomi supervise Guru in her place because while the blonde was wary of both of them, she was clearly not as intimidated by Naomi. Despite their currently not optimal terms, Naomi was never one to turn down a genuine request from a family member. It had taken almost a week for the two women to agree on where and when the lesson should take place.

Enjay decided to watch as well out of boredom; she had been sitting around the apartment all week with nothing to do. After all that was figured out, Guru's lesson began.

"I suppose the most logical place to begin is a brief overview of general Essence, then it may be easier to explain my way of manipulating it..." Guru blushed in embarrassment after she realized she was mumbling.

She cleared her throat nervously and began. "Imagine Essence being similar to white light; it contains all *colors* within it. Now think of an individual's soul like a stained glass window, only allowing certain colors of light to pass through. These *colors*, as I called them, can be shaped to become different forms of magic that can be manipulated from the user's own slowly replenishing supply of Essence."

"That's why different people are better with certain types of magic, right?" Eliza questioned.

"Yes." Guru confirmed. "But in theory, a mortal could train themselves to use all magic... it's just never been done."

"What about immortals, then?" Naomi asked curiously.

"I... do not know for certain." Guru admitted apologetically. "I'm aware that they draw power from Creation, the primary immortal that never changes, rather than from within a soul, but the details I'm unsure of. Mistress never bothered informing me."

"Fate." Kira corrected her gently. "She's not the boss of you."

Guru pursed her lips. "Ah... right... I-"

"And don't say sorry. You did nothing wrong." Kira grinned kindly at the shorter, young woman.

Guru looked away from the brunette, her cheeks rosier than usual. She smiled slightly. "O-oh..."

Eliza abruptly cleared her throat, snapping Kira and Guru out of whatever trance they had put each other into.

Guru's head frantically snapped up, her eyes wide. "A-anyway, take a look around you, all of you. It's easiest to begin applying this magic to an area you're familiar with. Every detail should make it easier to activate this magic, so please take your time and observe. For you, Miss Eliza, I recommend trying to use your other senses to observe. That... should help, I think." Her voice dropped to an unsure whisper by the time she was done.

Naomi decided to try it and see if she'd be able to use Guru's form of magic; it wouldn't hurt to have as a backup. She looked around, seeing a quiet, calm park area on the outskirts of a bustling city. She saw her cousins, eyes open and darting about and lips pursed in concentration. Guru had leaned against a nearby tree, her face scrunched up in thought.

"And once you're ready, close your eyes and reach out, not physically but try to extend your magic around you. Use the extended range to *feel* your surroundings."

She closed her eyes, the image of the area around her engraved in her mind, but after a minute or so... Naomi felt something inside her *change*, like someone flicked on a light switch in her brain that she had never noticed before. The image in her brain almost solidified.

The pink haired girl stood up, stepping out of the way of the others though her eyes were still firmly closed. She walked out into a smell in the forest clearing that she had only seen walking here.

"Yes yes!" She heard Guru gasp excitedly. "Excellent, Miss Naomi!"

Naomi sensed a presence come up behind her, someone that felt like the mandated tranquility of a silent library.

Guru let out another little cheer. "Brilliant, Miss Eliza!"

Naomi raised a brow, wondering if everyone had such a specific sensation linked to their soul. But she had little time to consider the question as she heard her cousin's breath hitch slightly.

"I... know where I'm going..." Naomi felt the relief radiating off her cousin. "I know where I'm going again."

"You all did quite well! Better than I expected!" Guru smiled proudly, clapping her hands together quietly, but enthusiastically.

Despite the praise, Kira looked disappointed. "But... I couldn't do it."

"You cannot expect yourself to master every type of Magic, Miss Kira. Some of us are simply not attuned to certain types of magic. For example, this is the **only** type of magic I can effectively utilize." Guru replied gently, putting a hand on the brunet's shoulder. "Besides, I could sense how hard you were trying... such effort is in itself admirable."

Kira blinked, seeming a bit surprised at the compliment. "D'you really mean that?"

Guru nodded bashfully. "I swear on my prophecy rank, I do."

Kira bit her lip, trying to hide a touched smile. "... Thanks, Ru."

"You swear on your *rank*?" Naomi cut off the interaction a bit more demandingly than intended.

Guru's eyes widened. She hastily retracted her hand from Kira's shoulder. "Ah, yes. I am aware that my rank is quite unimpressive, but-"

Naomi shook her head. "I get what a prophecy rank is, but why does it matter? We're all members of prophecies, aren't we?"

Guru pursed her lips. "Has no one explained to you?"

Kira and Naomi shook their heads.

Eliza shrugged. "I have inferences, but that's it."

"I know what they are." Enjay replied bitterly. Naomi raised a brow at her sudden switch in attitude, but said nothing.

Guru gave her a sympathetic glance. "Ah. You find your rank less than ideal?"

"That's none of your business." The amourite responded harshly.

Guru apologized, quickly backing off. "W-well... for those of you who do not yet know, let me explain: in a deck of cards, certain cards are more valuable than others, yes? The prophecy deck is no different. It is said that those with higher rankings are more important... less disposable."

Kira and Naomi shared a look.

"Uh... people aren't *disposable*." Kira grimaced.

"In the eyes of the majority, you would be told you are quite incorrect." Guru responded meekly, clearly worried they would get upset with her for saying as much.

"Okay, that's a **whole** different issue that we probably can't unpack right now." Naomi sighed. "So is it just the card value, or is there more to your rank?"

Guru seemed relieved at the shift in topics. "Suite matters as well. Hearts are the most prestigious, representing notable bloodlines, followed by diamonds which represent abundance, whether it be strength, worldly riches, magic or something else entirely, and then spades which represent persistence and hard work... and finally clubs... which represent circumstance."

"Are we ranked very high, then?" Naomi questioned.

"You are, Miss Naomi. Out of this group, you have the highest ranking in this group as the Jack of Diamonds. The Jack symbolizes a protector."

"Aw, no fair. Why does Naomi get the cool one?" Kira pouted teasingly.

Guru shook her head. "Your ranking isn't obscene, Miss Kira. You sit with a middling rank as the Seven of Spades. The Spades represent grit and hard labor, as I said. Numbers do not hold specific meanings other than rank based on numerical order, but seven is considered a number of power."

"Huh." Kira shrugged. "That doesn't seem bad... I can live with that."

"How do you even know our rankings?" Naomi frowned.

Guru looked down. "I did tell you that Mis-Fate had me memorize The Deck, did I not?"

Naomi nodded slowly. "Right, yeah."

"What about Lizzy and Jay?"

Eliza growled. "Kira, use my damn name or I SWEAR TO-"

"Sure thing, *Elizabeth*."

"I hate you."

Enjay looked up, clearly confused. "What did you call me?"

"Jay?" Kira repeated questioningly. "It's... a nickname."

"A *what*?"

"I'll explain later." Naomi cut in. "But it's not a bad thing."

"Um..." Guru bit her lip, shifting her weight from foot to foot. "I'm uncertain of why Miss Enjay is unsettled, but Miss Eliza and I have fairly low rankings..." she admitted shamefully.

Naomi shrugged nonchalantly. "Okay, so?"

Guru looked surprised for a moment before subtly shaking her head to herself. "On Sonoria, if you were a part of The Prophecy Deck, you were treated based on your rank. Admittedly, I don't recall much of my time before becoming Fate's servant, but I do not look upon my remaining memories favorably."

"I know from... *past events* that I'm The Three of Hearts." Eliza grimaced. Naomi quickly put together that she must have learned it from reading Lierra's mind based on how uncomfortable she sounded in admitting it.

Guru nodded. "Miss Eliza is slightly saved by her card suite, however."

Enjay let out a groan. "I'm The Ten of Clubs... seriously, not even a face card."

"A-actually, despite the suite, a ten is a very reputable-" Guru gulped at the icy glare Enjay sent her and moved on with a shaky smile.

"I'm the second lowest card in the entire deck... The Three of Clubs." Guru chuckled bitterly. "Clubs represent circumstance... or more ironically in my case, **fate**. I am but a commoner caught up in unorthodox circumstances."

Enjay looked conflicted, her expression wavering between disgust and understanding. Naomi was admittedly darkly intrigued by her reaction.

"How is that possible? Aren't you pretty involved in all this prophecy stuff?" Naomi questioned.

"Level of involvement and rank often do not correspond." Guru explained. "Yes, I may be quite involved, but that does not equate to my importance."

To Naomi, that just sounded like a sad excuse to be prejudiced against other people, but she doubted bringing that up to Guru would do much other than make the shorter girl uneasy. "Alright, I think that's enough about prophecy stuff for a while. Let's just go home."

"You're quite the looker." Fate smirked as she dragged a finger across the other immortal's chest. "You're truly beautiful, you know."

"I should hope so." He replied smoothly, not looking up from his book. "We immortals are the idealized self images of our mortal hosts, after all."

"Yes, Blue was certainly attractive." Fate admitted easily. "But he was nothing compared to you."

He leaned over, giving her a quick kiss on the lips before languidly rising to his feet. "I must oversee preparations."

Fate sighed in frustration. "If I still had Guru, we could just send her to check."

"We mustn't focus on the past, *ma bijou*." Knowledge reminded her calmly. "We have more than enough capability without your runaway servant."

Fate's eyes narrowed. "I know that, it's just... ***vexing***."

"Just consider the possibilities of what servants you'll have after we succeed. You won't bother thinking about that puny girl any more."

Fate hummed in agreement. "Will you be long?"

"Of course not, darling."

Fate smiled widely. "Come back soon and maybe I'll have a *present* to give you." She winked flirtatiously.

The corners of the immortal's mouth quirked upwards. "Is that so? Well then, I'll do my best to hurry."

After their magic session, Kira had dragged the girls off without a second thought, wanting to show Enjay and Guru what life outside of the apartment was like.

Naomi was surprised how amazed Guru was, especially considering the fact that she went with Kira to get groceries once or twice before.

"These humans look so... personalized." Guru explained to Naomi upon seeing her questioning expression. "In Sonorian culture, clothes are not chosen to add personality, they are simply to show others your status. Mistress treated them similarly, having me wear the robes of a priestress."

"It was like that on Amour too." Naomi's eyes widened at that. Enjay was pretty talkative, but she always seemed to avoid the topic of her past like a plague.

Enjay caught Naomi's stare, but didn't elaborate, instead changing the subject. "How do you get those?" She inquired, motioning to a large pair of feather earrings worn by an especially pretty girl across the street from them.

"Piercings?" Naomi clarified. "You could ask our resident piercings expert." She nodded at Kira, who grinned proudly at the title. She even motioned to her nose ring as proof of her expertise.

Enjay stared at Kira for a second, looking rather surprised. "Can you get them anywhere?"

Kira shrugged. "More or less. I know a good place in town if you want some."

Naomi side-eyed her cousin warily. "Kir, I'm not sure if that's the best idea-"

"No, I... want to try it." Enjay cut her off with a decisive nod.

Eliza sighed. "At least I won't have to *see* you turn into a second Kira."

"Rude." Kira muttered under her breath, turning to Guru. "What about you, Ru?"

Guru's eyes widened, she was clearly not expecting to be included in the conversation. "W-what about me?"

"D'you want piercings too?" Kira's voice became much more gentle as she addressed the shorter girl.

"I..." Guru pursed her lips before frowning pensively.

"You don't have to." Kira reassured her. "They're permanent, so it's totally alright to take your time deciding."

Once again, Guru was shocked by her words. "But I... get to choose?" Even Eliza looked up in surprise when the namu said that.

Kira blinked. It took her a moment to process Guru's reaction. "I mean... yeah. **You're free now.**"

Guru looked down, clearly having a hard time comprehending all the information supplied for her.

Naomi opened her mouth to say something, but Kira beat her to it. "How 'bout this: we start off with something temporary, like your clothes, and we work our way from there?"

Guru carefully eyed the outfit she was wearing. Her current outfit was one of Eliza's graphic T-shirts and lounge shorts, so they were quite baggy on her. "You... are not offended if I choose not to wear this?"

Eliza shrugged. "I don't care about clothes. I just wear whatever fits; can't expect everyone else to be as practical, can I?"

"I... suppose not." Guru smiled slightly. "In that case, perhaps I should try... freedom of expression."

Naomi felt her suspicion for Guru dwindle. She didn't even feel in control over her own clothes, which made it hard to internally blame her for choosing to be with Fate.

"So... *how* exactly did you get this kind of money?" Naomi asked, feeling uneasy as she discreetly eyed the price tags on the dresses in front of her.

"Eliza." Kira answered a little too easily.

"Uh-huh." Naomi frowned, turning to Kira's sister. "And where did *you* get it from?"

Eliza chuckled mysteriously. "That's my secret."

Okay, not suspicious at all. Naomi internally sighed.

"I like places like this." Kira said after a few seconds of silence between the three. "I wonder if life before the war was like this." She motioned to the shop around her.

Naomi tensed. "Kira..."

"I know, I know. We're not supposed to bring it up." She huffed in annoyance. "I was just thinking out loud. Is keeping all hush-hush suddenly some sort of *implied* law now?"

"I mean... kind of?" Naomi answered slowly. "You know we gotta keep things under wraps. There are still magic traffickers and Anti-Mages out there." Naomi never understood her cousin's nonchalance about this; Kira's own grandfather had been an Anti-Mage, so why was the brunette so blasé about the war?

Kira rolled her eyes, exasperated by the moot point, but said nothing in return.

You know what would happen if people knew magic users were still here. Was the unspoken reminder that hung over them.

Luckily, Enjay came out of the changing room, smugly handing Naomi a hefty pile of various clothes. "These fit."

Naomi blinked, sending the petite blonde a glare over the nearly *endless* heap of clothes. "I carried Eliza on my back for **miles** not that long ago and this pile is somehow more heavy."

"What can I say? I need clothes that better suit my *beautiful* body. Besides, I grew up broke, so I'm making up for lost time." Naomi was more than a little shocked that the confession slipped out, but it was pretty obvious that she wanted to pretend she never said anything when Kira asked for an explanation.

"Urm... Miss Kira?"

Kira whipped around, almost knocking Eliza over at the call. Eliza snickered, despite nearly being pushed onto her butt.

"Yea-" She stopped herself, her face turning red. "Oh... WOW."

Guru pursed her lips. "Is this... unacceptable?" She asked worriedly.

Naomi could only see part of Guru, given the **giant** pile of clothes in front of her face, but what she was able to see was much more of an alternative aesthetic than she would have expected.

"You almost match Kira, now." Naomi noted, almost amused.

Kira somehow managed to pull off a look that was simultaneously alternative and reminiscent of a dad on vacation. She liked to wear a black sleeveless shirt under a loud, open button up or flannel with loose pants and dark combat boots, something she could move comfortably in and still have a distinctive look about her.

Guru blushed, clearly embarrassed at the comparison. "O-oh... is that bad?"

"Nah, you two just look like a couple now." Naomi smirked.

Guru squeaked in alarm, her face turning red. "I... f-forgive me, Miss Kira! I never meant-"

"N-no, you look **great**- I mean good. You look good." Kira looked away, clearly flustered.

"Would y-you rather I cha-"

"**NO!** I mean... no, it's fine..."

Eliza, appearing to be getting tired of the mutual pining, stepped in. "Weren't we here for Enjay to get her ears shot?"

"*Excuse* me?!" Enjay clearly didn't notice Eliza's sarcasm.

Naomi nudged her arm to get her attention. "She doesn't mean it... sort of."

Enjay frowned. "Then why-"

"It was a joke, **relax**." Eliza sighed tiredly.

Enjay's indigo eyes narrowed. "Oh... so how do I-"

"I'll show ya'." Kira grinned, practically dragging the smaller girl away. "I know someone in the back who's been doing this for years!"

After watching as Enjay followed her cousin, Naomi trudged over to the front counter (thank Sonoria there wasn't a line). She used Eliza's mystery money to pay for everything, calling for Guru and Eliza to follow her back home.

"Blossom..." Z looked at his sister-in-law hesitantly.

"Hm?" She blinked at him curiously.

"How long does it take Fate to... uhh... you know... enact punishment?"

Blossom gently closed the book she had been reading, pausing for a moment to think. "I thought she could track Essence signatures, but... if that was the case, she would have found me long before I had time to settle down and discover the true consequence for using forbidden magic."

"That's because she used me as her scent hound. I would sometimes... bend the truth of where her victims were located to give them more time."

Blossom inhaled sharply, whipping around in her seat to see Guru nervously standing in the doorway.

"Oh! Guru! How... how long have you been here?" Z asked, clearly caught off guard.

"We just got back." Naomi grunted, dragging Enjay's new clothes packed in an industrial sized bag behind her.

Blossom immediately relaxed at the sight of her daughter, but the calm was short-lived. "Wait... **what did you do to Kira?** Where is she?!" Blossom glared at Guru, who visibly wilted in fear.

Naomi's eyes widened. "Mom, **nothing** happened to Kira..."

"Enjay's getting piercings. We got bored waiting for them, so we came back first." Eliza elaborated coolly.

"Oh." Z smiled. "Okay then." The explanation was enough to satisfy him.

"**No**, it's not 'okay', Z! I thought the namu was teaching you magic..." Blossom's frown deepened.

"She was. We just went shopping afterwards." Naomi stared blankly at her mother, not understanding why she looked so tense. "I can protect them; you don't need to be like that."

Blossom's eyes narrowed. She was silent for a minute or so before responding. "Fine, but let me know where you're going next time, at least."

Naomi nodded curtly, turning to Enjay and Eliza's room to drop off Enjay's haul.

20

The next few months seemed to drag on for Naomi. Blossom and Z were still in agreement not to go after Blue, keeping as low of a profile as possible in the process, which was a bit hard when living in a two bedroom apartment with six other people, but they managed.

Naomi's birthday came and went. She had to admit, spending it with her mother was nice, even if they were still not on the greatest of terms with each other. The family entered a rather monotonous rut that Naomi knew she needed to break from. She didn't care if her mother forbade her from doing so, she was going to save her brother. So she began to plan, deciding to sneak off on her own in the middle of the night, so she couldn't be followed (except by Guru, who would only realize she was gone once she was too far away to go after).

Finally after months of agonizing waiting, Naomi waited until she was sure everyone was asleep before silently picking herself up and creeping towards the front door. Her mind was made up; she had laid out a note for her mom and uncle so they wouldn't come after her. All she needed to do now was leave the apartment without-

"What are you doing?"

Naomi had to harshly bite her tongue to keep herself from screaming out in frustration. "Oh... Enjay... I'm just-"

Enjay's indigo eyes shifted down and fixated on the messenger bag slung across Naomi's torso. "Oh. You're leaving?" She sounded far too relaxed at the possibility.

Naomi pursed her lips. "Well-"

"Can I come?"

Naomi hadn't expected that. She stared at the blonde in confusion. "Wait what?"

"I'm not used to staying in one place for this long. I need some action. So... can I?"

Naomi wanted to scoff at her gross misunderstanding of the situation. "This isn't a vacation, Enjay."

Enjay sent her an annoyed look. "I know, I'm pretty, not stupid. You're going after your brother, right?"

Naomi blinked. "How- no never mind, did Kira tell you?"

Enjay shook her head. "It's not very hard to tell; you were obviously going to go after him eventually."

Naomi's shoulders sagged. Was she really *that* obvious? "Look, there's no reason for you to-"

"There is." The blonde pressed. "I want to help."

"Enjay-"

"I want to prove to myself that I can."

Naomi bit her lip pensively. Enjay wasn't family, but Naomi still felt the need to protect her after finding her freed from her immortality. She really didn't want to let her come along.

Enjay could see Naomi wasn't convinced, so she continued. "I won't just be a dead weight. I can be useful. I have survival skills and I'm good at making quick decisions... *oh*! I'm also **really** good at persuading people to do things!"

That caught Naomi's attention. "What do you mean you can *persuade* people to do things?" She asked skeptically.

"Well... I'm not completely sure." Enjay shrugged. "Ever since I was little, I was just naturally good at convincing people to do stuff... it was really useful until people started resenting me for using it as an ***unfair*** advantage."

Naomi blinked. "Is that your magic?"

Enjay's face scrunched up almost enviously. "I can't use magic, I've never been able to. Learning that kind of stuff is a bit hard when all you do is try not to starve to death all day. But I'm still useful!"

Naomi looked away for a moment. *She really wants to help... maybe she sees this as gratitude for saving her or something... I should be able to watch over just her, it should be fine... probably.* "Alright, you can come." Naomi sighed. "But **please**, don't do anything that would compromise the mission."

Enjay grinned. "Wouldn't dream of it! Let's go!"

"Ah, before you do..." Guru quietly stepped out of her room, Kira and Eliza close behind. "May we accompany you as well?"

Naomi's blood ran cold. Of course Guru was still awake, just her luck.

"But... don't you guys hate Blue?" She questioned her cousins, trying to get them to change their minds.

"Oh definitely." Kira nodded. "I'm doing this for **you**, not him! Besides, this way, I can kick his ass after saving it! He'll never live it down!" She slammed her fists together with a wide grin.

"I mean... I definitely don't like him, but I don't wanna sit back and do nothing, you know?" Eliza replied.

"There's no way to change your minds, is there?" Naomi frowned.

Kira, Eliza and Guru all shook their heads.

"If you are **completely** sure, then fine." Naomi looked at them scrutinizingly, trying to sniff out potential liars from the pack. When she found none, she sighed and begrudgingly backed down.

"Then let us go!" Guru smiled excitedly.

21

Knowledge sighed, waiting until Fate was a considerable distance away before checking his pocket watch.

He had ten days before he was done with Fate, but if everything remained on schedule, the Reality Ripper should be complete in half that time.

He couldn't help but feel a sense of satisfaction at the precise timing he had so elegantly created for himself.

He had no doubts that his plan would come to fruition. **He** had conceived it, after all. Between his intellect and Fate's sheer power, there were no obstacles he saw as a valid threat.

The only issue he could predict was if his mortal counterpart's sister came into the picture, which she no doubt would. Of course, a mere mortal stood no chance against him, but her presence could shift Fate's motivation towards anger fueled revenge, which could prove troublesome.

But it mattered not. Either way, with or without Fate, he would succeed.

"So... what's the plan?" Eliza asked pointedly.

Naomi pursed her lips. "We save Blue."

"Yeah, I got that part." Eliza scoffed. "What I mean is *how* are you planning on doing that?"

"Well... we find him?" Naomi frowned. "How exactly are we supposed to find an immortal though? Any ideas?"

"We could locate his sanctuary." Guru supplied. "Every immortal is granted one."

"But... where would it be?" Enjay deadpanned, grunting as she shifted her heavy backpack; Naomi put her foot down and made her carry her new stuff by herself.

"If his sanctuary is anything like Mi-Fate's, it would have sentimental connection to his mortal self. Creation enjoys adding details along those lines to their immortal subordinates."

"Fate's had sentimental value?" Kira frowned.

Guru nodded. "Yes. She told me offhandedly that the cliff overlooking the sea was where she first arrived on Earth."

"But Blue doesn't remember his past like Fate, does he?" Eliza frowned.

"That wouldn't matter. Creation couldn't care less if he truly remembers or not. They do everything for their own amusement, and they find the irony of manipulating the sentimentality of their immortals entertaining." Guru answered, turning to Naomi. "Is there any place Mister Ex-Vaden would consider special?"

Naomi's expression darkened. "Yeah. I can think of somewhere like that." She answered in a low voice.

Guru nodded. "Perhaps we should see if his lair has manifested there."

Naomi exhaled slowly, adjusting her backpack pensively. "I don't wanna go back there, but if I have to... I will... for Blue."

23

"Here we are." Naomi announced in a low voice, gesturing to her old home from before Fate uprooted her family and entire life.

Guru frowned. "I don't sense any abnormalities in Essence here, but perhaps he used a cloaking spell of some sort?"

"Might as well check." Eliza shrugged. "Worst case scenario- he's not here and we get to camp out in the house tonight."

Naomi seriously didn't like that idea. Yes, she had been using the house before, but without Blue, it seemed off, even if he didn't know she was there, in the first place.

Naomi took the lead despite her discomfort. She marched up to the front door and looked back at Guru. "You don't happen to know if using the front door is a trap, do you?"

Guru pursed her lips. "It's... possible, but not likely."

Great. Naomi internally sighed. She psyched herself and turned the handle.

To her surprise, it was unlocked. The door opened to show her the living room of her old home.

"Ah." Guru cautiously stepped inside and took a quick look around. "It appears this is indeed not his sanctuary."

Naomi felt a bit defeated. Where would Blue's sanctuary be if not their old home?

"Well, we tried. I call the master bedroom." Eliza walked away, staying close to the walls in case her magic malfunctioned. She had gotten better at using it over the past few months, but was still growing used to it.

"HEY! You can't just-" Kira was cut off by Eliza slamming the door behind herself.

Naomi stared at the place Eliza had walked from. "That room was locked shut last time I was here. How did she-"

"Maybe someone unlocked it?" Kira shrugged. "I mean, I don't think it matters that much. Let's just think about it in the morning."

Naomi didn't like that idea, but she nodded all the same. "There are two more rooms and four of us."

"I'll share with Guru!" Kira blurted out.

Guru stared at her with wide eyes. Naomi looked at her suspiciously.

"I... I mean... sharing is the only way we'll all fit, right?" The young woman laughed nervously as she hastily backtracked.

Naomi gave Guru a quick glare. "You better not do anything *raunchy* in there." She threatened darkly.

Kira spluttered. "**NAOMI!**"

Guru squeaked in alarm, her face red. "I-I understand!"

Naomi grunted in acknowledgement, taking mercy on them and toning down the fear factor. "Blue had a wider bed. Mine won't fit two people."

Guru nodded her head rapidly as Kira pulled her down the hall.

"If that girl does **anything** to Kira, I swear to Sonoria-" Naomi's grumbling was cut off by Enjay clearing her throat impatiently.

"Oh. Uh... you can take my old room. I'd rather not lock myself in there again, so I'm fine with the couch."

Enjay shrugged, her expression slightly surprised. "Suit yourself." She walked off towards the last bedroom.

Naomi, however, didn't go to the couch. She crept out of the living room and into the dining area, looking for something, *anything* that could help her save her brother.

When she found nothing out of place, she went into the kitchen, where she immediately spotted a note on the kitchen counter.

She peered down at it, picking it up after recognizing her brother's handwriting.

She read it without hesitation.

Naomi,

I probably won't ever see you again, but I promise that I'll fix every-thing. I met someone who can help me bring back our parents.

Naomi cringed at the mention of Iona.

But in case I have to resort to Plan B, I want you to know that I never forgot about you. I-

There was a mess of illegible lines, like someone startled Blue while he was writing. Naomi had to skip down to the end of the paper.

I don't have enough time to write down everything I want to tell you, so just remember that I'm doing this for us.

If you ever need to find me, just think of Alice.

-Blue

Naomi blinked, rereading the note to make sure she hadn't missed anything.

Alice? She wondered. *Who's- oh.* **That** *Alice.*

If Naomi remembered correctly, Alice was Blue's first girlfriend. Naomi hated her with a burning passion, especially after she cheated on Blue on his own birthday, right in front of him.

Naomi, however, had absolutely **no** idea what Blue meant when he said to think of her. Naomi avoided Alice after the pink haired girl saw her flirting with some poor red haired boy who was **way** too infatuated with her for it to be healthy.

Naomi carefully folded up the note, stuffing it into her bag.

She knew she couldn't figure it out now, but maybe, with luck she'd remember in the morning.

24

Naomi didn't remember anything when she woke up.

Well that was misleading to say, she did, but it was all just nightmares of the night her mom was taken from her, not anything she wasn't already aware of or could be deemed as important to the task at hand, so she reinvigorated her illusion to cover up her imperfections and got on with her day.

Naomi took the note from her bag and reread it again, turning when she noticed her older cousin's unsuccessful attempt to sneak up on her.

"Morning, Kir." Naomi smirked, not looking up from the note.

The older girl threw up her hands in frustration. "EVERY TIME!" Kira huffed. "How did you know?"

Naomi chuckled. "You're not very good at being quiet. Your breathing is too loud."

"*Everything* about you is too loud." Eliza corrected with snark. Kira glared at her sister, even though she couldn't see it. Eliza was smart enough to expect the response, anyhow.

"Actually... Miss Kira is quite a silent sleeper." Guru whispered timidly, cautiously emerging from the room she and Kira shared.

Naomi finally looked up and leaned over the back of the couch to stare analytically at the freckled girl, making her shift her weight nervously from foot to foot.

Kira whacked Naomi upside the head playfully. "Dude stop it, you're scaring her."

Naomi sighed, going back to rereading Blue's note for the thirtieth time that hour.

The action caught Kira's eye. "What's that?" She pointed at the paper.

Naomi shrugged. "Blue left it on the counter. Wha- GIVE IT BACK!" She demanded as Kira snatched the note out of her hands and scanned over it.

The brunette's face contorted into a grimace. "Oh... *Alice*." She practically vomited out the name in disgust.

Naomi blinked. "You know Alice?"

Kira scoffed. "How could I not? She pretended she was bi just to get access to my magic. Not an uncommon occurrence, that's like *half* of my dating history, but still!"

That caught Naomi's attention. "She dated Blue for the exact same reason." Naomi recalled.

"Apologies, but... what are we talking about?" Guru asked meekly.

Naomi's thoughts were coming together. She had to ignore Guru to maintain her train of thought. "Kira, was there anywhere important she took you? Maybe somewhere Blue would have known?"

"I mean... she broke up with me in the old library outside of town... so maybe there? She took me there a few times."

Naomi nodded, eagerly grabbing her bag. "Then let's check it out!"

"Okay but-" Kira was cut off by her stomach growling at them all. She chuckled, embarrassed. "Let's eat before we go."

25

The library was deserted, but Naomi could tell that it wasn't yet abandoned. Certain books were separated into piles, none of which were covered in dust.

The realization made her feel a twinge of defeat. If this really was Blue's sanctuary, he would have made sure that no one was able to waltz into his personal space so easily.

"Guru, do you sense anything?"

The purple eyed girl shook her head. "There's not enough residual Essence here to warrant anything of note, even a concealment charm."

Naomi felt her eagerness completely deflate. *I guess this place wasn't the right one, after all. If only- Wait...* Naomi spotted a small piece of paper lying on an otherwise empty table.

She tentatively walked over to the table. *Is that... Blue's handwriting?*

She picked up the paper, reading it, albeit more skeptical this time.

Naomi,

If you actually found this, I'm sorry to tell you that this isn't the place you're looking for.

If I had to pick anywhere to make a sanctuary for myself, I'd go somewhere you wouldn't expect me to be, just so you wouldn't find me there from just a glance. A library isn't exactly a strange place for me to be.

I don't like leading you on like this, but Iona keeps looking over at me, and I'm worried she'll read the notes if I make them seem important.

Don't get me wrong, I love her, but I always have a Plan B.

-Blue

Naomi grit her teeth, her grip on the paper tightening, almost ripping it. Of course Blue saw her as a backup plan. He only wanted her to find these if his initial plan failed, she was stupid to hope for otherwise.

"Second place, huh?"

Naomi jumped, instinctively backfisting whoever was behind her in the face.

The intruder of her personal space yelped and let out a string of garbled curses.

Naomi turned sound, blinking in surprise. "**Enjay**! Don't get in my personal space like that!"

"You BROKE MY DAMN NOSE!" Enjay glared at her.

"Sorry!" Naomi grabbed her hand instinctively. "It's a habit!"

"No, she didn't break it. It's just bruised." Guru noted, making them all turn and stare at her curiously.

"What?" The blue haired girl seemed slightly put off by the sudden extra attention. "I can read unconscious thoughts with great concentration. The physical body can tell me a lot, you know."

"Okay that's great, can we PLEASE get back to how to fix this?!" Enjay pointed at her face, which was bleeding aggressively.

"I know a bit of healing magic." Kira noted. "I haven't really practiced... ever, so I might set your face on fire or something, but it's worth a try."

"I'm sorry, *WHAT*?!" Enjay all but screamed.

Kira laughed sheepishly. "Well... when light magic backfires, it tends to change into thermal energy, so..."

"Okay, you know what? Just do it." Enjay interjected. "I'd rather have a burnt face than one with a crooked nose." Her voice was far too serious for Naomi to even think she was joking.

"Wow. Dramatic much?" Eliza deadpanned.

"Your choice." Kira shrugged, walking over to her and placing a hand on her forehead. Her eyes squinted in concentration and Enjay's bruising nose began to glow, but luckily, no flames erupted.

Kira backed away, grinning proudly. "First try!" She whooped, patting herself on the back.

"Good job!" Guru applauded softly. "She's not even singed!"

Enjay stared at them incredulously, but bit back another string of curses she no doubt had prepared.

"Now that *that's* out of the way." Eliza spoke up before anyone could interrupt. "What do we do now?"

Kira was the first to speak up. "I guess we think of somewhere Blue wouldn't usually go." She shrugged.

"But there are **tons** of places that Blue wouldn't go!" Naomi remarked pessimistically.

"It's somewhere you should know, Miss Naomi. Perhaps that narrows the selection down?"

"But it also needs to be somewhere with emotional sentiment to him, right? Do you know anywhere like that?" Enjay asked open endedly.

Naomi slowly turned to Enjay, trying to conceal how impressed she was that the blonde actually remembered.

The shorter girl scoffed as she recognized the taller one's surprise. "I know I look like a blonde bimbo, it's only natural when you look this good, but I'm not *completely* incompetent."

Naomi stared at her blankly for a moment before turning to her cousin. "Eliza? You taught her the word 'bimbo'?"

Eliza shrugged. "I taught her a lot of words. I don't know."

With that out of the way, Naomi quickly switched back to her single minded objectivity. "But... I can think of somewhere he might be." Naomi grimaced.

Guru perked up. "Where?"

"The place where we met Fate for the first time... when she took away our mom."

26

After a few minutes of walking in tense silence, Kira couldn't take it anymore. "If we're gonna walk for miles, can we at least **do** something other than internally debate the meaning of life?!" The brunette exclaimed frustratedly.

Guru's eyes widened. She gasped a bit from the sudden shattering of the silence. "W-well... what do you suggest we do in that case, Miss Kira?"

"We're not doing 'Never Have I Ever' again." Eliza grunted.

Enjay stared at Eliza curiously. "Is the name anything like the actual activity?"

"That's basically **all** it is." The blind one deadpanned.

The indigo eyed girl grinned widely. "Oh, we should **definitely** do that, then."

"Eliza already voted against it." Naomi reminded her, effectively settling the debate before it even began.

"You guys are no fun." Kira pouted teasingly. "Can we please just do *something*?"

"We could take turns answering each other's questions." Guru suggested hesitantly.

"**Yeah!**" Kira eagerly agreed, making Guru smile at her accomplishment.

"Sure." Eliza shrugged. "As long as it's not a 'Never Have I Ever' format then I'm down."

Enjay thought for a moment before agreeing. "Well… if you all are going to find out about me, I'd rather it be on my own terms, so why not?"

"No." Naomi stated firmly. "No chance in hell."

"Come on, dude!" Kira pleaded. "I won't ask anything bad!"

Answering questions about herself was one of the social requirements Naomi hated doing most. But even so, Naomi glared at her cousin, relenting. "I'm not answering anything personal."

"Fine by me!" Kira beamed at her success. "First question: Guru, what's your deal with calling my dad by our last name, but not any of the rest of us?"

Guru seemed just as surprised at the inquiry as Naomi felt. "Have I been doing that again? I sincerely apologize; I never meant to come off as impolite!" She hurriedly assured them. "I was simply… raised to address men in such a way." She looked down in embarrassment.

"What does that mean?" Enjay raised a brow.

"On Sonoria, in the era I was raised at least, it is-was viewed as more respectful to address someone with their given name instead of their family name… in acknowledgment of the individual, but men were… how do I put this-"

"Secondary?" Naomi supplied.

Guru shifted nervously, giving a brief nod. "I really do try to not say such things… or even *think* such things, but one of the frustrating aspects of being reset is having to break all of your bad habits over again."

Kira blinked. "Oh. I thought it was more of an accident, if anything."

"May I…" Guru bit her lip pensively. "May I ask you a question, Miss Kira?"

"Yeah, it's your turn!" Kira encouraged.

"Well…" Guru paused, trying to find the best words to structure her question. "I was wondering… why was 'coming out' such a fear inducing act?"

Kira stared at her blankly for a second before very confusedly responding. "'Cuz... not everyone's cool with it?"

Guru shook her head. "Ah... that wasn't quite what I meant to ask. More so, I wanted to know **why** you specified."

Once again, Kira looked incredibly confused. "Uh... so people know? Because it's important to me? So my dad stops trying to set me up with guys? Take your pick."

"I think... this is a cultural difference." Naomi observed when Guru's frown only deepened.

Guru let out a small "oh" of acknowledgement. "That is what I was wondering. No one really says such things on Sonoria. You simply courted who interested you, there were never... words to describe one's preferences. I take it Earth isn't like that?"

Eliza chuckled and shook her head. "**Everything** has a label here." Naomi couldn't exactly disagree.

"I see..." Guru paused for a moment to process. "In that case, I am under the same label as Miss Kira." The blonde smiled to herself. "Saying it in such a direct way is... *affirming*. It's rather unnecessary in my mind, but... I don't mind it."

"Sweet! Lesbians unite!" Kira cheered.

Guru tilted her head curiously. "Is that the word? *Lesbian*?"

"Yeah; one of them, at least!"

"Oh... a nice sounding word..."

After a moment of quiet, Guru seemed to realize that her turn was over. "Um... Miss Eliza! C-can you successfully do any types of magic, excluding what I taught you and your mental abilities, of course."

Eliza thought for a minute. "I mean... I can hypnotize people, but that's kinda in the realm of 'mental abilities'."

Kira stared at her cautiously. "When have you *hypnotized* anyone?"

Eliza smirked. "I got you to give me your snack stash last week, didn't I?"

Kira gasped in over dramatic horror. "So that's where my chips went! You **traitor!**"

Guru smiled slightly at the exchange. Naomi hadn't really ever seen her express amusement before, it was almost sweet seeing her progress.

"I'll go with Enjay." Eliza continued, barely skipping a beat once Kira had recovered from the horrifying discovery.

The blonde blinked, looking over at the blind girl expectantly.

"Some stuff you offhandedly mentioned earlier got me thinking... why can't amourites express themselves through appearance?"

"Self expression is imperfect." Enjay answered automatically. "Anything imperfect is done away with."

"Like... random example... having one eye?" Naomi asked cautiously.

Enjay stared at her incredulously. "Naomi, the singular scar on your wrist is imperfect, **of course** missing an entire part of your face would be considered imperfect!"

"I was just asking!" Naomi defended.

Enjay sighed, continuing after a beat of silence. "That's why I'm so proud of my beauty... back home, that's all I had."

Naomi gulped at that. *Could that be why my grandfather...*

Enjay snapped out of her momentary daze. "Anyway! Naomi, I've been wondering this since I noticed your appearance flickering,"

Kira turned her head, looking at Naomi frustratedly. Naomi tensed slightly.

"Why do you constantly cover yourself in illusion spells?" The blonde finished. While unsurprised, Guru still curiously looked up at her, Eliza simply raising a brow.

Naomi pursed her lips, trying to seem as unbothered as possible. Luckily, she was rather good at lying. "I don't know what you're talking about." She answered coolly.

"That's a lie." Eliza immediately added without even looking up.

Naomi internally cursed herself. How had she been stupid enough to forget that her cousin was a walking lie detector?! "Well either way, I already said that I'm not answering personal questions."

"Is your little secret more important than us?" Kira sent her a side glare. Her eyes flashed cyan for a moment. Guru gently rubbed the brunette's shoulder, calming her down.

"It's not that!" Naomi denied indignantly, offended that Kira would even think such a thing. "It's just..." Naomi looked away, trailing off.

"We don't think you're weak, Naomi." For the first time since Eliza lost her eyesight, Naomi felt her cousin's gaze boring into her.

Naomi flushed. "I never said-"

"That's what you're thinking. I don't need magic to see that much." Eliza grimaced at her own choice of words. "Well, not *see*, but you know what I mean."

Enjay chose to say nothing, opting to nod awkwardly with what the blue haired girl was saying. She obviously didn't have much experience in situations like this.

Naomi didn't reply to either of her cousins, simply picking up her pace a bit to make it look like she had moved on from the conversation.

"So..." Eventually, Enjay's discomfort from the silence got the better of her. "what's the plan?"

"I'll remind Blue of who he truly is." Naomi responded quickly.

Enjay frowned at the simplicity of the idea. "Will that work?"

"The only reason Miss-Fate retained her memories is because that was her wish when she became immortal." Guru supplied quietly. She looked away before continuing. "I... do not think simply reminding an immortal of their previous existence will suffice." Her tone served as an implied apology.

Naomi couldn't help but grow frustrated. "Well, I don't hear any other ideas." She snapped coldly.

Guru gulped, slowly exhaling, like she had just come to terms with something horrible. "Miss Naomi... I could..." Guru frowned nervously, silently deciding to start over. "If Knowledge has the Forbidden Book in his position, I will-"

"**NO.**" Kira cut Guru off harshly, shaking her head before the young woman could finish. "Out of the question."

Enjay blinked confusedly. "What?"

"Guru's offering herself as a… trade-off of sorts." Eliza summarized.

"I am simply offering," Guru continued earnestly. "Miss Kira, Miss Naomi, I am indebted to you two, so I would be perfectly willing to-"

"You already said that you don't want to be immortal." Kira cut her off again, her eyes turning an electric hue of cyan once more. "You're **not** sacrificing herself. You hear me?"

When Guru saw the shift in Kira's demeanor, she shut down completely. She offered no reply other than a shaky nod.

Naomi felt disgusted that a small part of her was actually considering Guru's offer, but she pushed the feeling down, focused on what was ahead of her.

27

"We're here." Naomi felt a wave of nausea roll through her as she stepped into the clearing. She had a terrible feeling that her theory of Blue's sanctuary being here was right. "Guru?"

The girl closed her lilac eyes, her face pinching in concentration. "I feel... *something*. It could be a protective seal."

"How do we know if this is the right place? There's not a door or anything we could check." Enjay pointed out.

Guru nodded. "That is the point. Sanctuaries are not easily accessible. My Mis- I mean Fate had her entrance over the edge of a cliff. One had to jump into the water below to enter."

"So we just... wait for something to happen?" Kira frowned. "That doesn't sound right..."

"The entrance should appear or we should be transported inside once we prove we can enter." Guru replied.

"How do we do that? I assume it's not jumping off a cliff again." Eliza inquired.

Guru shook her head. "It wasn't the cliff that allowed us to enter. It was an act of putting one's life in the hands of fate that managed to allow us within. The rules for entering sanctuaries are dependent on the immortal they belong to."

"How do we know what immortal Blue would be, though?" Naomi frowned deeply.

"Well, he was searching for information, according to Mi-Fate, so he likely became Knowledge as a call upon what he sought after."

Kira hummed thoughtfully. "So... do we list off the Periodic Table of Elements or something? 'Cuz if that's the case, we're out of luck. I suck at Chemistry."

Guru shook her head. "No no, nothing like that. Fate taught me how to enter each immortal's sanctuary in case of a diplomatic emergency. To enter Knowledge's space, something only known by one must be shared to another."

"Oh. We just share a secret?" Kira sounded slightly disappointed. "Isn't that... too easy?"

Guru shrugged. "I suppose it depends on the individual."

"Okay, who's willing to share?" Eliza officially questioned. "I'm out."

"So am I." Enjay stated firmly.

"I don't have anything that only I know." Kira chuckled awkwardly. "I'm a pretty open book."

Naomi and Guru looked at each other silently for a moment.

Guru broke the interaction, looking at her feet. "I... volunteer."

Naomi internally let out a sigh of relief.

"In all honesty, I was saving this for a memorable moment, but I suppose now will suffice." She took a breath before continuing, turning to fully face Kira. "I... everyone I've ever met in my three millennia of existence has conditioned me to be someone else, a servant, a slave, a pet, but I have never... met someone who has wanted me to just be myself." Guru smiled slightly, her cheeks turning pink. "Until I met you, Miss Kira. So... thank you. I know this is... not as dramatic or exciting of a reveal as you all probably anticipated, but..."

Kira pulled Guru into a tight hug, causing the unprepared girl to squeak in alarm. After she had processed what was happening, she hesitantly returned the gesture. "We do not do this on Sonoria. It is... quite nice."

As the two hugged, Naomi saw something glow out of the corner of her eye. She turned to see an illuminated circle on a large, nearby rock. As soon as her fingers brushed against it, the circle within the glow vanished, revealing a long, rusted ladder.

"I guess we climb down." Enjay said for everyone.

Kira grimaced, suddenly remembering. "Eliza, if you can't-"

"I have the magic Guru taught me." Eliza cut off her sister icily. "I'll be **fine**."

Naomi wanted to disagree, but there was a level of finality in Eliza's expression that made Naomi see her as silently threatening. She bit back a retort. "I'll go first. Eliza, you go last, so you can take your time."

The blue haired girl sent her a glare, but nodded curtly. "Fine."

28

Naomi couldn't help but notice the books that began to surround her the further down the ladder she climbed. They were all thick, in perfect condition and different from their neighbors, each a distinct color and size.

In fact, the further she climbed, the more aware she was of the space opening around her. The ladder shifted and swiveled, like those she had seen in old movies and television shows when she was younger. The discovery made her climb slower and more cautiously, as to not scare those above her with unexpected movement.

She continued to climb, now completely surrounded by books on all sides, but a promising glow beneath her encouraged her to keep moving.

She climbed for what felt like hours; her hands were raw and bleeding and her legs were beginning to tire, but she pushed through it all, solely focused on her brother.

After another eternity of climbing, she reached solid ground. She stepped off the ladder and looked around, silence and her companions as her only visible company.

She was in what looked like a giant library, with nothing but books, papers and folders filling endless shelves. There wasn't a visible ceiling, just an unexplainable glow not unlike fluorescent lighting far above her.

As she looked over the space for a third time, her eyes locked onto something- or rather someone, who was definitely not there before.

Naomi held in a gasp as she saw a slightly more mature, certainly taller version of her brother. His skin was much paler and porcelain than it had previously been, but not in a sickly way, his hair was shoulder length, jet black and tied back into a neat ponytail. He wore a crisp, pinstripe suit with a strikingly crimson tie that was the only color on him other than his cold, metallic, gold eyes that were focused on a book he was carefully reading. He sat in a plush, velvet armchair that was an unorthodox shade of mauve, but it oddly suited his new look.

His eyes lifted from his reading material. He gently closed his book to stare analytically at Naomi with an almost bored expression.

His presence wasn't nearly as suffocating and radiant as Life's or Fate's, which admittedly, sparked some hope in her. "Blue..." Naomi couldn't help but call out.

The immortal sighed quietly, standing from his seat and adjusting his tie. "No, my dear jack. Not anymore."

"Naomi, did you-" The words got caught in Kira's throat as her eyes moved up to observe all eight and a half feet of the immortal before them.

The immortal's gaze shifted to the brunette. "The powerful demon spawn. Liberated from yourself... or are you?" He whispered cryptically.

Kira cringed, taking half a step back. "What is *that* supposed to mean?"

The black hair rolled his eyes, but offered no explanation, opting to instead address the others that had just finished climbing down the ladder. "Pretty little Class Five, have you finally attained the attention you were after?" He sent Enjay a calculated sneer.

The amourite was quick to bite back. "That wasn't what I was after and you know it!" She growled.

Knowledge raised a carefully angled brow. "Is one comment all it takes to affect you after all this time? How pathetic."

"Blue." Naomi tried desperately. "This isn't you. **Please**, come back to us. Come back to me."

The immortal tilted his head as he once again focused on Naomi. "Do not try to reawaken your brother. He is simply a part of me, and not one that you can access."

Naomi's eyes widened. "Part... of..."

The pallid man opened his arms. "I am **Knowledge the Infallible**, the keeper of history, the vast expanse of wisdom. I know what you plan to do, Naomi Serene Ex-Vaden. I know your past, I know your present, I know your brother, I know **you**."

A sick part of Naomi's mind took note that Guru was right in her claim that talking to him wasn't working. The rest of her did not care. All she wanted was to get her brother back.

"Your desires... your thoughts... your emotions all make you predictable, obvious, and most importantly, **boring**. There is nothing such a bland being could do to change me."

Kira's hands began to shimmer, her signature glowing knuckles appearing along the ridges of her fists. "Well, were you expecting *THIS*?!"

Naomi's eyes widened at her cousin's war cry. "Kira, **don't**-"

Kira lunged at the immortal, only to be calmly swatted away like a fly and sent hurtling into a bookcase a few yards away.

"KIRA!" Naomi screamed. Before she could do anything, Guru was at her cousin's side, helping her up.

Knowledge's expression never once changed. "Painfully foreseeable. I cannot fathom how they caused you such trouble."

Naomi froze as she realized who the man was talking to.

Fate emerged from the shadows, wearing her signature revealing shirt, leather jacket and ripped, black jeans. "Not all of us are as prepared as you, *mon ange*."

Guru stepped back in horror. Kira almost fell back over in shock as the weight supporting her shifted away.

"You flatter me, *ma bijou*." Yet, despite his words, Knowledge still sounded emotionless and hollow, which disturbed Naomi beyond words. This... *thing* had the same face and voice as her twin, but acted like a twisted, stoic machine.

Fate ignored the mortals before her for a second, taking her time giving the male immortal a heated kiss, taking care to sneer at Naomi as she intimately touched what used to be her brother.

Naomi balled her fists and forced down the incredible urge to lurch forward and punch out Fate's perfect, white teeth.

"You can't have him, little jack, he's **mine**." Fate said, hungrily staring at Knowledge, who was still, even after such a passionate moment, was emotionless as before.

"Yet they will not leave without what they seek, as pointless as their endeavor is." Knowledge pointed out, wrapping his arms around Fate's tiny waist, not bothering to so much as glance back at Naomi.

Fate smirked wickedly, not taking her eyes off of him. "Then why don't we help them out?"

Knowledge only then turned to face them, gold eyes boring into Naomi's stony grey ones. "With pleasure." He smiled very slightly, detaching one arm from Fate and lifting it idly above his head.

Before Naomi could react, a strange, cloud-like gas emitted itself from Knowledge's hand. It didn't have a color or scent, yet it was so... beautiful.

Naomi grinned dazedly, her thoughts disappearing and being replaced with an unorthodox sense of serenity.

Naomi giggled deliriously, feeling nothing but giddiness as her body fell to the floor and completely shut down.

29

Kira inhaled sharply, her eyes snapping open.

What was she doing? She was forgetting something important.

She heard a quiet chuckle at her side.

The brunette turned to see her father, slightly older than how she knew him with more pronounced age lines and graying hair.

"Nervous?" He asked her, though his tone made the question sound almost rhetorical.

"For... what?" It was then where she noticed the crisp, deep green suit he was wearing, the clothes uncharacteristically well fitted and spotless. Her dad never cared enough about clothes to wear something so unnaturally *perfect*.

Z gave her a warm smile, gently looping his arm through hers. "You don't have to pretend, firefly. It's a big day for all of us." He hadn't called her that since she was seven. What was going on?

Kira frowned, her eyebrows pinching together. She was growing more confused by the minute, but somehow not alarmed or concerned.

A song reached her ears. Behind the door she and her father were in front of, someone was playing the piano.

"That's our cue." Z's eyes got a bit watery, but he was still genuinely smiling.

What?

The doors opened. There was a long aisle before her and Z, and at the end of it, in a pitch black tuxedo that gorgeously hugged her curves...

Kira's midnight eyes widened. "Guru?"

Sure, Kira liked Guru... and was more than a *little* attracted to her, but getting married seemed pretty sudden considering that they had only known each other for a short while.

Guru blushed at the sight of her, offering a small, bashful wave. "Y-you picked a beautiful dress. It really... suits you."

Z walked away and sat down in the front row of... wherever exactly they were, some sort of outdoor venue on a beach. Had she just imagined walking through a set of double doors?

Kira looked down, surprised to see that she was indeed wearing a dress. She wasn't a dress person most of the time, but if she really felt like making a statement, she'd make an exception to her otherwise strict 'pants only' policy.

And this wasn't just any dress. She was wearing a long, flowing, elegant mass of crisscrossed fabric showing off her toned abs and shoulders, along with her dark blue gem of a belly button piercing that her mom had so ardently hated when she saw it for the first time. Even the anime tattoo on her ankle, which not even Naomi knew about, was proudly exposed since she wasn't wearing shoes.

"You don't look too bad yourself." Kira offered, hoping to calm the shorter woman's nerves. It seemed to work, just a little.

"I announce you two as officially wife and wife."

Kira almost jumped in surprise when she realized there was another person on the stage with them. And, wait a minute, did he say-

"You may now kiss your bride."

Guru's glance shifted to the audience before focusing back on Kira. Her blush deepened. "I'd much rather our first kiss be in private, but..."

Kira felt her face heat up. She leaned towards Guru, gently connecting their lips together.

Guru was nervous and Kira was unprepared, so the kiss didn't last long, but Kira found herself craving more as they parted. Guru's lips were soft and warm, coated with a bubblegum scented chap stick.

Everyone in the audience cheered.

"I now introduce Kira Ivy and Guru Vaden!"

Kira couldn't help it, she burst into a smile. She felt Guru beaming beside her.

The reception started in a blur. Kira dimly recalled talking to a few people, but she honestly didn't remember who they were or what they said in the slightest.

She was just enjoying the party until... she saw her mom.

It felt like everything froze.

Lierra was gone. She couldn't be here. She was **dead**.

"You can talk to her." Guru offered softly.

Kira stared at the freckled young woman in shock.

"We have the rest of our lives together." The blonde explained with an almost bashful grin. "You're more than welcome to talk to your mother for a few minutes."

Kira nodded. "I'll be right back." she promised.

"I don't doubt it. I trust you." Guru smiled. "Take all the time you need."

She whipped around and ran as fast as physically possible in her long, flowing dress.

Lierra perked up upon seeing her daughter, halting her conversation with some lady Kira didn't know. "Kira! I was just- **ooh!**" The words were abruptly stopped by the sheer force of Kira's bear hug.

"**Mom!**" Tears were shamelessly pouring from the brunette's eyes.

Her mother gave a strained laugh. "Hun, you know I love you, but you're making it a bit hard to breathe."

"Oh! S-sorry!" Kira quickly let go.

Lierra noticed her crying. "Is being married finally settling in?"

"It's just... you're **here**... I thought you..." Kira couldn't bring herself to finish that sentence.

Lierra smiled warmly, gently brushing away her daughter's tears like she used to when Kira was little. "Of course I'm here! I would never miss my little girl's big day!"

Was everything from before... a dream? Lierra felt so **real**. This all seemed so... **alive**. This **had** to be real.

"S-so you're okay with... Guru?" Kira asked cautiously.

"Oh sweetie." Lierra nodded. "All I want is for you to be happy. We worked out our... *past*. And I don't care that she's a woman. As long as you're happy, I'm happy. I know you've dreamed of getting married for a long time, my little firefly."

More tears fell. Tears of pure joy.

Kira embraced her mother tightly once again, promising herself to never again let go.

Never.

***

"What d'you think, Liza?"

Eliza's eyes hurriedly opened and she shook her head to help wake herself up. "Huh?"

Kira was staring at her with wide, expectant eyes. Eliza had almost forgotten how dark and blue her sister's eyes were.

Wait. Eliza saw her... her eyes...

Eliza shakily brought her hand up to her face, turning it over and over in disbelief. "I... **see** you." Saying it made her believe it even more. She had her sight back.

Kira stared at her blankly. "Uh... yeah? That's how eyes work? D'you, like... need a break or something? I know your insomnia is a serious bitch sometimes."

Eliza opened her mouth, but closed it again, unsure of how to reply.

"What... are you doing in my room?" she settled on asking.

Yes, this was **her** room in **her** house, not that crappy, old apartment in the city.

Once again, Kira looked confused. "Do I really have to repeat it?" Kira chewed her lip, expression becoming conflicted. "You're helping me with our homework; remember?" She begrudgingly admitted in a whisper, her cheeks flushing in embarrassment.

Eliza stared at her older sister blankly. "But... you never want my help with anything, much less academia."

Kira let out an awkward chuckle. "Yeah, well... as much as I hate to admit it, you're the smart sibling... so..." the brunette rubbed the back of her neck self consciously. "and besides, mom wanted us to spend more time together."

Eliza froze. "... Mom's here?" It took every ounce of willpower she possessed to keep her voice from breaking.

"Well **duh**!" Kira grinned brightly, but after seeing her sister's watery eyes, the gesture fell. "Eliza? Are you... seriously okay?"

Eliza nodded. "I just had a very... *realistic* dream. It doesn't matter now. Let's get back to your homework."

***

"Madam, I apologize for the disturbance, but you have visitors."

Enjay's eyes lazily opened.

She soon realized that she was sitting on a... throne? In the middle of a room decorated with white gold and royal purple emblems?

She peered over her throne to see a young woman clothed in emerald robes kneeling at her feet, head lowered respectfully. "Who..."

"Two middle aged amourites, one man and one woman. Would you like me to send them away?"

No. Something inside her commanded. "N-no, no need... send them in."

The servant nodded, ushering in a small man white a white blond head of hair and matching stubble with a tall, pallid woman holding his arm lovingly, her deep, indigo eyes looking intently at Enjay.

"I will be outside if you need me, Milady." And with that, the young woman briskly left, closing the magnificent, gold doors behind her, leaving Enjay alone with her parents.

Enjay's eyes glued onto them. "How... Mama? Pa?"

The woman smiled, her eyes sparking with pride. "Enjay, darling..." tears were pooling in her radiant, almond shaped eyes.

Pride... Enjay stared at her parents in shock. *They're... proud of me?*

"What are you two doing here?" The blonde couldn't help but ask.

Her mother didn't reply. She just took a few steps forward, her bright expression growing with happiness. "You look so beautiful."

Enjay blinked. She looked down at herself, quickly realizing that she was much taller with a more hourglass figure covered in pale satin and jewels. Was this her immortal form?

"But Mama-"

"We wanted to see you, Enjay." Her father finally spoke, his pale blue eyes shining with the same sense of pride as his wife's. "And thank you."

He spoke?

Why did that seem so miraculous?

Her mother nodded in agreement.

"*Th-thank* me?" Enjay repeated doubtfully. "For what?"

Her mother chuckled softly.

"Don't act like you did nothing, love." Her father grinned, amusement evident in his voice.

"What-"

"You restored my status." Her mother filled in, taking her husband's hand and caressing it fondly. "You gave me another chance... you gave **us** a chance." She finished, gesturing to her hand, which was still intertwined with her husband's.

Enjay opened her mouth to respond, but no words left her mouth.

"You made us proud." Her father added fondly. "So proud."

"You're... not mad I left?" She asked in a small voice.

Her parents shook their heads.

"It was for the best." Her mother said decisively.

"We should have let you search for a better life a long time ago."

Enjay's lip trembled. "I didn't even say goodbye..." That was her biggest regret. She had left, yes, but she always remembered leaving her parents without even an explanation or word of farewell.

Her mother smiled sadly, walking up the steps to Enjay's throne. "Darling..." she wrapped her daughter in a warm hug. "**We forgive you.**"

We forgive you... her parents **forgave** her. They were **proud** of her for taking charge of her own life.

Enjay tightly hugged her mother back, a smile spreading across her pallid face.

***

Guru gasped softly, a rush of warmth grabbing her hands. She looked down to see heart covered, well manicured fingers gently caressing the backs of her own freckled hands.

"Mis... tress?" Guru was well acquainted with Fate's alternative form, since she so often used it to seduce and manipulate people. But, Guru was the first one... the first she *knew* of, that fell in love with Fate like... ***this***.

There were tears being held back in Fate's emerald doe eyes, her long lashes just barely concealing the crystal droplets of water.

"Is... something the matter?" A sense of fear rose up in the blonde. "D-did I do something ***wrong***?"

"Guru..." The red haired siren sighed deeply, a large tear rolling down her pink cheek. "Guru, no. You've done nothing wrong... in fact, I'm the one who's wronged you."

Guru frowned. "What... do you mean?" She asked hesitantly.

Fate once again fondly rubbed the back of Guru's hand with her thumb. "I used you..."

"Mis-"

"Let me finish." Fate implored. "**Please**."

"O... okay..." Guru nodded slowly.

"I forced you into a role you were too precious for... I constantly disregarded you and toyed with your emotions, I experimented with your body... and I did it all over and over for millennia. You never deserved that."

Guru's jaw couldn't help but drop. "Are you... **apologizing**?" It seemed too good to be true.

Fate smiled sadly. "I am."

She looked away, guilt clouding her expression. "But, does it really even matter, in the end? It doesn't change anything."

"Yes, it does!" With a sudden surge of confidence, Guru reached out and gently guided Fate to look back at her. "That... was all I ever wanted to hear." Guru beamed, tears now escaping her own eyes.

Fate stared at her with wide eyes full of disbelief.

Guru continued to smile, gently rubbing away Fate's tears with her thumb. "I just wanted you to acknowledge... and apologize."

"Guru..." she leaned closer. Guru had almost forgotten how intoxicating Fate's honey sweet scent could be.

"Yes Mistress?"

Fate shook her head. "**Iona**. My name is Iona."

Guru froze. Fate had never trusted Guru to call her by her real name before. "*Iona...*" she whispered, still in shock.

"I know this might be a few millennia late, but..." Iona laughed anxiously. "late is better than never."

Guru inhaled sharply at the red haired young woman pulled her close, so close that their lips were grazing each other.

"***I love you***, *mon ange*."

Guru turned red as Iona left a trail of gentle kisses down her neck, leaving her to process the words she'd fantasized of hearing for so long.

She wanted nothing else. She felt truly happy.

***

Naomi was confused.

She woke up only to find herself under a tree. Why was she sitting under a tree? Had she been napping there?

"Mimi!" The old nickname snapped her out of her thoughts. She looked up to see Blue grinning down at her.

Blue... Blue was **here**.

But that's impossible. She thought. *Blue is-*

"Kira wanted your opinion for a new tattoo idea." Blue rolled his eyes in exasperation as he relayed the message. "She wanted you to design it, this time."

Naomi automatically shook her head. "She shouldn't get another one. Aunt Lierra's still mad about her septum piercing she got last week." The words spilled out of her mouth before she could process them.

But wait... the septum piercing argument was only last week? Didn't that happen six months ago?

"That's what *I* told her." Blue agreed. "But she doesn't want to hear it from me."

Naomi probably should have expected that. Kira was never the biggest fan of her brother... for some reason.

Huh, why couldn't she quite remember why?

No, it wasn't important. Not right now.

The tan young woman sighed, getting up and stretching her arms. "Okay, I'll go talk to her. Where is she?"

Blue pointed behind him.

Naomi almost dropped back to the ground in shock. "Our... house?"

"Uh duh. Where else would we live?" Her twin asked, his voice dripping with sarcasm.

Naomi couldn't help but smirk at the snarky reply. "Okay *genius*, where's Kira?" A strange but welcomed air of playfulness washed over her.

"Your room." Blue answered. "Watch your step in case Liza's reading on the floor again."

"Will do." She set off in search of her cousin.

As Naomi marched into the house, she let her smile drop.

Something was off. Wasn't she just doing something else? For whatever reason, her memory of what she was doing before was hazy and distorted, like it was nothing more than a dream, but it felt **important** and she couldn't remember why.

She kept the instinct in the back of her mind, but she tried to focus on what was ahead of her... literally in this case.

"Uhh... Dad, what're you doing on the floor?"

Her dad? Wasn't he not supposed to be here for some reason? Naomi couldn't put her finger on what gave her such a feeling. Seeing him was filling her with euphoria... but why would it? She saw him everyday... right?

"Oh hi, Mimi." He chuckled awkwardly, getting up from his previous position of laying with his stomach to the floor. "It's, uh... a long story." He motioned to the floor and back up to his face as some type of poorly thought out explanation.

"Do I *want* to know?"

"It has to do with your aunt smacking me in the face on a bet, so..." North shook his head. "Probably not."

Naomi rolled her eyes, giving her dad a quick side hug before continuing on her way. The feeling of suspicion she had grew.

There was a thought somewhere deep inside her telling her to pause and look around, find her Aunt and question her personally, but she ignored it and continued on her way.

This isn't real.

Naomi froze. She was near the end of the hallway. A voice that sounded suspiciously like her own seemed to whisper the phrase in her ear.

No... it has to be real. Naomi denied, looking back at her hands. *It feels real, so-*

Then where is your scar?

"My... scar?" Naomi's blood ran cold.

Very shakily, she slowly brought her right hand up to her face. She turned her wrist a couple times, seeing nothing but untouched skin. "N-no..." she shook her head vigorously in horror. "**no...**"

This isn't real.

Please... I just want my family...

You have to break free.

I don't want to.

Despite her thoughts, the ground around her got dimmer, almost dissolving into off colored gas.

No!

She desperately looked up, trying to find whatever force was pulling her out of her idyllic reality. "Don't make me go back there..." Naomi cried one last time, pushing every ounce of desperation in her into her voice to try and keep herself where she was.

I'm sorry.

Naomi's world went dark.

30

Naomi didn't want to wake up. She so desperately tried to resist it and lull herself back into her dreamworld, but it was pointless.

She opened her eyes to find her face streaked with tears. She hated when anyone saw her cry, but there was nothing she could do about it now. Knowledge was already staring at her.

She looked up to see Knowledge staring at her with a mildly interested expression, like a scientist reading his experiment's results for the second or third time, picking up new fragments of information. "The result, I expected completely, given your experience with illusions..." he very thoughtfully stroked his bare chin. "but your reaction..."

"What even was *that*?!" She snapped, trying to sound braver than she actually felt.

"My power, harnessed to create a full bodied and encapsulating illusion." The immortal responded nonchalantly.

"But Blue can only use-"

"A singular, individualized form of magic, yes." Knowledge finished with an exasperated sigh.

Blue could influence electric signals in his brain, allowing him to learn things faster and remember more than most people. He couldn't express his magic outwardly, but it was convenient since he loved learning so dearly.

"As I said before, I am not your brother. I am... *more* than Blue Ex-Vaden." The immortal concluded.

Naomi tried to move, but she was bound by some invisible force, freezing her in place. She grit her teeth, glaring up at him. "Why are you doing this?" She asked in a low, dangerous tone.

"I was ordered to." He replied stoically.

Before Naomi could fully process what he said, he turned away from her, facing a vast, open area in front of him.

They were no longer in the library. They appeared to be in some massive cave. There was glowing, bluish fog illuminating the whole area. The fog kept close to the ground, except for when it circled around Knowledge, as if it was coming from him. At the edge of the cave, there was a large, iron archway that was completely empty. The light of the fog seemed to be almost repelled by it, leaving a gaping, almost unnatural shadow.

Naomi shook away the unease she felt looking at the arch. "Where are my friends?" She demanded.

Knowledge didn't bother to face her as he responded. "Why don't you look for them?" He invited, vaguely motioning around the cave. "Perhaps they moved."

He snapped, Naomi's body jerking forward as her continued efforts to just move finally got somewhere.

Naomi got up, about to summon a club or blunt object to knock the immortal out.

"I wouldn't try that if I were you." He said calmly, his back still facing her as he readjusted his cuff links.

Naomi froze. *How did he-*

"I know how you think, Naomi Serene. You cannot surprise me."

He turned his head just enough for Naomi to catch a glance of his gold eye staring down at her. It made her blood run cold. "Now if you excuse me, I have business to attend to." Before Naomi could even open her mouth, the immortal's form dissipated, dissolving into a cloud of glowing gas that sank to the ground.

Naomi stared at the vacant spot where Knowledge disappeared, taking a few beats to confirm that he was really gone. As soon as she had accepted that he was no longer there, she bolted in a random direction, desperately looking for any sign of the people she came here with.

31

Kira laughed as she spun Guru around, the shorter girl giggling and blushing.

"You're so beautiful, you're glowing." Kira observed fondly.

"Of course I am! I have you with me, *Mistress*!" The word sent a wave of jealous and pity through her, but almost as soon as she felt the searing feeling-

Kira blinked. "What... did you just call me?"

Guru stared at her in confusion. "Kira?"

"A-are you sure? I could've sworn-" she cut herself off. She wanted to enjoy her wedding. "Never mind. I think I misheard you."

Guru nodded slowly, still looking fairly confused. "How strange... I just had such a weird thought..."

Kira frowned, not liking this shared feeling of... *strangeness*. "What was it?"

Guru looked her directly in the eye. The brunette felt almost unnerved at the sudden intensity of her wife's lilac eyes.

"How did we meet?"

Her mouth went dry. "How we... met?"

That's when everything shattered... **literally**.

The walls turned to glass, everything crashed, wedding guests gasped and yelled before evaporating into thin air.

Kira's eyes widened. She looked around in horror

THIS ISN'T REAL!

Kira stepped back in shock. Was that Naomi's voice?!

"What-"

WAKE UP!

"WAI-"

***

"Kira! It isn't real!"

"Naomi-"

The pink haired girl was yelling too loud to hear. "WAKE UP!"

"Nao-" she was cut off by a searing pain across her face that flung her head to the side. "DID YOU JUST *SLAP* ME?!"

Naomi blinked, hesitantly lowering her hand. "... Are you awake now?" She asked almost doubtfully.

"**YES** I'M AWAKE! WHAT DID YOU THINK I... was... wait, where are we?"

"Still in Knowledge's sanctuary, I think." Her cousin was frowning pensively.

Kira sat up, looking around, suddenly alarmed. "Where's-"

"You're the only one I've found so far."

Kira blinked owlishly. "... *Found*?"

"Yeah..." Naomi bit her lip as she helped Kira up off the ground. "Whatever you were just experiencing was an illusion, a really powerful one, at that. I've been looking for you guys for a while now, but the fog makes it hard to see everything."

"But..." Kira grimaced. "Guru was there."

Naomi stared at her in blatant disbelief. "What?"

"Yeah, she was my-" Kira slapped a hand over her mouth, her face completely red. "she was there..." she finished lamely.

Naomi raised a brow but, much to Kira's relief, didn't ask. "I've... heard full bodied illusions like what Knowledge gave us can be connected between consciousness... so it's possible..."

"We need to find her." Kira realized, a feeling of dread creeping into her chest. "She called me Mistress. I think she might be..."

Naomi paled, instantly picking up on what Kira was implying. She grabbed her older cousin's hand. "Come on. The fog changes color closer to body heat. We should be able to find Guru, Enjay and Eliza if we keep an eye on the gas."

Kira glanced down. Naomi was right, around them both, the fog had become more pale purple than blue.

Kira nodded. "Lead the way. I don't wanna go in the same direction you came from."

32

"*Ma bijou...*" Knowledge offered the feminine immortal a slight smile. "it is almost time."

Fate grinned darkly, fondly stroking her whip. "Perhaps there are realities out there in need of my **justice**... when the transport is ready, what will you do, *mon ange*?"

"I know everything here." Knowledge acknowledged. "I yearn to know everything outside of this reality as well."

Fate hummed thoughtfully. "Sounds like you have a long journey ahead of you."

Knowledge chuckled slowly. "And what would you do if I agreed with you?"

Fate snaked her hands around the taller immortal's waist, smirking seductively. "Why don't I ***show*** you instead?"

***

"Purple mist!" Naomi pulled Kira towards the fog in question, swatting it away as much as she could, only to reveal Eliza sitting on her knees with an absolutely defeated look on her face.

"Eliza?" Kira asked with a quiet gentleness that Naomi had never heard from her cousin.

The brunette's younger sister looked up. She wasn't crying, but she looked like she should be. "I could **see** again, Kira." She gave a pained smile. "For a second, everything was **perfect**... but I knew it was wrong." She made no move to get up.

"I think... that was his plan." Naomi started slowly. "He wanted us to be distracted, even after the illusion had lifted." She internally debated how to best get Eliza to start moving. Naomi didn't know how much time they had until Knowledge or Fate would come back.

"He did a good job." Eliza chuckled bitterly. "His impression of Mom was horribly realistic..."

Naomi pursed her lips. "Eliza-"

"It was, wasn't it?" Kira kneeled down to be about the same height as her sister.

Naomi shook her head at Kira. *Stop. This isn't going to-*

Trust me. Kira's eyes implored. *I know what I'm doing.*

Naomi exhaled slowly, looking away begrudgingly.

"But... I think we're stronger than his tricks." She offered Eliza a small grin. "I believe in us."

Eliza looked down, smiling slightly in reciprocation. "Yeah..."

"So let's get up and show him what we're made of!" Kira encouraged, pulling her sister up.

Naomi couldn't help but stare at the two of them almost longingly. Maybe in an ideal world, she and Blue would have been able to reassure each other like that.

33

They found Enjay next.

Naomi immidiately set to work on trying to snap Enjay back to reality like she had with Kira, but Enjay was extremely resistant to Naomi's intervention of her illusion. Naomi had to try to pull her away from the fantasy land, like she had done to herself.

"NO!" She remembered the blonde shrieking. "I FINALLY MADE THEM PROUD! DON'T MAKE ME GO!"

That cry had made Naomi freeze.

Kira and Eliza, of course, urged her to try to free Enjay from the illusion again, but Naomi realized something in that moment. "She's holding on too tight... I don't think it's possible to pry her away without loosening her grip on the illusion more directly."

Kira frowned. "How exactly are we supposed to do that?"

Naomi turned to her younger cousin.

Eliza paled. "No." She immediately shook her head.

"Eliza-"

"I'm NOT going into her mind, Naomi! Guru *wanted* me to! She can't even consent to it!"

"How else are we supposed to snap her out of it?!" Naomi argued.

"I don't know!" Her younder cousin scowled. "Go into her illusion or something!"

Naomi blinked. "Is that even possible?"

Eliza bit her lip and shrugged. "I mean... I read about it once, so... maybe?"

Naomi sighed, walking over to Enjay. "Okay, fine. I'll try it, but if it doesn't work-"

"I'm **not** changing my mind, Naomi." Eliza laid out with a grimace.

"Okay..." She sat next to Enjay's unsettlingly still form, which was sitting and facing the opposite way.

Alright Enjay. It's just me. Let me in. She closed her eyes, focusing on Enjay's slow breathing as everything faded away.

***

Naomi opened her eyes, gasping quietly when she found herself in front of two large, gold doors in an equally large, luxurious hallway decorated with royal purple banners and rare gems.

She glanced down to see that she was wearing green robes that were touching the floor, her hair kept out of her face in a half-up style not unlike how Guru had her own as Fate's servant.

It worked. Whatever she just did had worked!

She cracked open the immense doors just enough so that she could see into the room she was in front of.

Inside was a giant throne room decorated with luscious purple and gold embellishments. There was a woman standing up from the cushioned throne who looked suspiciously like-

Naomi inhaled sharply. *Lady Life.*

Life was hugging a middle aged woman with coppery skin and rich, long, black hair. She was most certainly gorgeous, and only slightly more so than the slightly shorter white blond man with expressive sky-blue eyes standing next to her.

Could these two be... Enjay's parents? Naomi frowned at that; they definitely looked the part. *She did mention before that she never got closer with them...*

Breaking her from the fantasy world would probably be harder with sentient imitations of her parents preventing her escape.

Life broke away, sighing quietly. "Sage, you can come back in here, now."

Naomi blinked. *Sage? Is she talking to me?* The pink haired woman followed her instinct and pulled open the heavy doors, walking back up to the immortal. "Yes, Ma'am?"

"Introduce yourself to my parents. They'll be my honored guests here, for the time being."

The woman blinked. "Oh Enjay, you don't have to-"

"It's my treat, Mama." Lady Life cut her off fondly.

"Let our child have her moment, my love." The man rubbed his wife's back reassuringly.

"**Exactly**! Pa has the right idea!" The immortal's grin widened.

The raven haired woman smiled knowingly as her daughter puffed out her lips and pulled out an especially effective pair of puppy eyes. "Well then, I suppose..."

"I'm Sage, Missus and Mister Ellis. It's my pleasure to finally meet you two." Before Naomi could wonder what to do, she instinctively bowed in respect. It seemed to be the right choice given how Lady Life nodded subtly in approval at her greeting.

"Oh, she's beautiful, Enjay!" The black haired woman gushed. "What a pretty face. There's amourite blood in her, isn't there? She had such a nice body type too! It's so rare to find such well balanced hourglass figures these days!."

Naomi wasn't exactly sure how she was supposed to respond to *that*. "Uhh... thank you-"

"And such stark grey eyes! Enjay, darling, are those contacts?"

Enjay, or maybe Life looked over, staring at Naomi for a minute. She looked like she was caught off guard. "No... that's her natural color..." Though she seemed hesitant in her answer, almost like she had just noticed.

Actually, even as Enjay's mother rambled on, Enjay continued to stare at Naomi almost nervously. She must have begun to realize that Naomi wasn't supposed to be there.

"Missus and Mister Ellis, do you mind if I spoke with your daughter in private for a moment?" Naomi cut in.

"Oh?" The dark haired woman raised an eyebrow, but nodded slowly. "I suppose... come along, my love." She gently pulled her husband out into the hallway.

Life was staring at her with an increasingly apprehensive expression.

"You..." The blonde started nervously. "you didn't look like that before... you didn't have a name."

"You're right." Naomi wasn't entirely surprised. Having a servant likely wasn't a huge aspect of Enjay's illusion, so it was less defined as a result. "That isn't natural." The gray eyed girl wanted to break it to her slowly, considering how desperately Enjay was clinging to the illusion. "You must know that."

Naomi wasn't used to seeing an immortal's gold eyes so utterly lost. "Who... why..." She didn't even know what to ask.

"You **let** me in." Naomi settled on starting with.

The immortal frowned in confusion. "What are you talking about? I haven't left my sanctuary in..." She trailed off, becoming panicked as she realized she didn't have a full grasp on what was happening. "I can't remember... why can't I remember?"

She's beginning to see that it's not real. Naomi noted. *But with that, shouldn't she be remembering things now? Maybe she's still holding on.*

"Sage," The goddess earnestly grabbed Naomi's shoulders. The pink haired girl felt the slight quiver coming from her pallid hands. "what's going on?"

"You may not like my answer..." Naomi responded cautiously.

"I need to know."

Naomi sighed. "I've been trying to free you for over twenty minutes; you know how long it takes people to snap away from illusions when actively pulled away from them? On average, less than two. **You're trapped, Enjay.** You're trapped and you don't want to admit it."

The blonde shakily sucked in a breath, letting go of Naomi with such speed that it felt like her tan shoulders burned to the touch.

"Enjay, **you have to let go**." Naomi told her in as calm of a tone as she could muster.

Small, almost insignificant cracks were snaking up the walls of the throne room. Whether the blonde liked it or not, she was waking up.

"Naomi..." That was the first time Enjay had said her real name since letting Naomi in her head. "I'm not ready."

Naomi took the pale girl's hands. "It's okay." She exhaled slowly, her voice soft. "You don't have to do it alone."

Enjay closed her eyes, giving a slight nod. "Then... I'm ready."

34

Naomi's eyes snapped open as she bolted up, her hand still firmly gripping Enjay's shoulder.

"Naomi!" Kira broke into a large, relieved grin.

"You sure took your time." Eliza muttered, covering up her concern with her usual dry humor.

Enjay had stood up with her, panting heavily with a strong look of defeat in her eyes. She was obviously upset that she was not able to say goodbye to her parents for a second time.

"Hey..." Naomi felt a strange bit of heaviness when she saw Enjay's saddened eyes. "I meant what I said. You're not alone, you know."

The blonde blinked owlishly at her, taking a few seconds to process the reassurance. She finally gave a slow nod.

"One more to go." Eliza noted.

Naomi grimaced. This would probably be the hardest one. "Guru."

***

Guru wanted to kiss Iona back so desperately, but it seemed **wrong**. Everything around her seemed **wrong**. This wasn't what-

"Guru?" Iona hummed, her grip around the smaller woman's waist tightening. "Is something wrong?"

Guru pursed her lips. "You... don't act like this."

"Guru..." The redhead grabbed her hands earnestly. "**I'm changing**."

"I've been by your side for over three thousand years... I don't understand why you suddenly feel the need to change for me after all this time." The blonde admitted gravely.

"I-"

"And I can't believe… this entire time I still have been focusing so much on you… that I forgot what I already found."

A switch flipped in Guru's brain, images flooded her memory. "I found someone who wants me to be happy for myself…" Guru's eyes widened as a name rolled off her tongue. "**Kira**…"

Iona's face suddenly darkened. "Guru…" Her voice became like Fate's, colder and more malicious. "do you not want me? Even after I changed for you?"

Guru froze. This had been exactly what she wanted, but… "I don't want you to change just to make me feel I owe you something… this is **my** life, Fate. I'm not living it just for you anymore."

As soon as Guru said what she needed to say, Iona's face began to crack, as if she was made of clay.

The woman gave her one last haunting glare as she shattered into nothing.

***

Naomi froze in her tracks. "Wait a second…"

Guru standing upright was looking up at something Naomi couldn't see. There was a single tear trailing down her cheek.

"She… broke out on her own?" Naomi was shocked. Eliza, Naomi could understand, but she could barely believe that Guru was able to pull away from her connection with Fate, even in an illusion.

"**HA**!" Kira beamed, running over to Guru and hugging her.

The sudden contact snapped the shorter girl out of her own head. "M-Miss Kira?!"

"You snapped out of it all on your own! Pretty badass! I knew you could do it!"

Guru's blush deepened. She smiled slightly, soaking in the words of praise.

Eliza rolled her eyes. While she couldn't see the lovey scene, her new magic was definitely cuing her in on what was happening. "Alright alright, break it up, love birds. We're not done yet."

Kira's face went red. Guru squeaked in bashful embarrassment, peeling herself away from the brunette.

Naomi took Enjay's hand, nodding slightly. "Let's go save Blue."

Fate exhaled slowly, watching in awe as Knowledgeable very carefully assembled the last of the archway.

He stood up, backing away to examine his work. He looked the large structure up and down, analytically staring at it and eventually giving a slight nod of satisfaction. **"It is done."**

Fate felt a thrilling rush of adrenaline pass through her. "How do we activate it?" She asked eagerly.

Knowledge produced a small control pad from his back pocket. "With this." He passed it to her. "Don't change the settings yet. The reveal deserves to be grand."

Fate admired the metallic device with a wide grin.

"Within the small compartment on the left, there is a glass orb safely stored. To activate the Reality Ripper, we simply pull it out and crack it, so the portal cannot be deactivated."

Fate blinked, frowning as she turned to him. "Why can't we deactivate it?"

"How else do you expect us to make a return if the portal closes?" Knowledge asked stoically.

Fate pursed her lips. "I suppose-"

"FATE!"

The immortal cringed in annoyance and disgust as she located the puny mortals challenging her.

"It never ceases to amaze me how much a single jack can get under my skin." The feminine immortal snarled.

The young woman completely ignored the immortal's comment. "Give me my brother back." Naomi demanded, her tone dripping with venom.

"That will not happen." Knowledge said idly, looking at Naomi with an almost bored expression. "I have consumed him. Not even his memories are in my possession any longer."

Naomi froze, but was only fazed by Knowledge for a second. "I don't believe you."

"Blue is gone." Knowledge repeated.

"Stop... LYING TO ME!" Naomi screamed, leaping forward and summoning a small pistol with her signature green magic.

Knowledge sighed, easily batting her away, making Kira and Enjay shriek in horror. It took Eliza a moment more to process what happened, but her reaction was nearly as severe.

Fate, however, was enraged. "Mon ange-"

Naomi groaned, shakily getting to her feet.

"There is no sense in combat. We will win regardless." He said emotionlessly.

"**Naomi!**" Eliza tensed, not entirely sure where to look. Enjay had bolted off before Eliza could follow her.

"YOU DON'T KNOW THAT!" Kira growled, her eyes flashing cyan threateningly.

Guru was quickly to grab the taller girl's hand. "Miss Kira." Her voice was quiet, but filled with enough force to keep Kira from throwing herself at the immortals looming over them.

"However," Knowledge continued as if he had never been interrupted. "to them, there is no alternative to fighting us in this situation."

"Well..." Fate grinned maniacally, summoning her signature whip. "let's give them a damn good fight, then."

Knowledge wasn't fighting, he stood on the sidelines and watched disinterestedly.

It was the five of them against Fate, but even with advantage in numbers, Fate had the advantage of power. Fate easily knocked them back, laughing as they practically threw themselves at her.

Kira had summoned her magic knuckles again and made a machete for Guru. Naomi still had her emerald gun and had just barely managed to toss a set of enchanted swords to Eliza and Enjay.

"This is pointless!" Fate exclaimed gleefully, her long fingernails suddenly extending into horrific, crimson talons. "Even alone, you puny mortals are but ants under my heel!"

As much as Naomi knew the immortal was right, some primal instinct deep within her kept her from accepting defeat. She had a small morsel of hope that something about their conflict would bring Blue back.

"BLUE!" Naomi screamed out, looking desperately at a clearly unmoved Knowledge. "I KNOW YOU'RE IN THERE!"

The immortal briefly looked up at her, making the young woman stop. The battle of their gazes began.

Knowledge smirked, his head tilting slightly to the left. "I've been told that my gaze can be quite... *petrifying*."

Naomi couldn't look away. Something was wrong. Her body wouldn't move!

"NAOMI!" Her cousin's eyes flashed dangerously as her attention turned to Fate. "You can't just-" Kira ran in front of Naomi, shielding her cousin from Fate. The goddess' attacks were relentless and unyielding, to the point where Enjay and Eliza quickly joined in, Guru leading the way. "Naomi, snap out of it! We can't hold her off much longer!"

Kira's observation was horribly right. Fate was forcing them further and further back, until Kira touched Naomi's side.

"No... I won't-" Another strike from Fate's whip cut the brunette off, making her quickly summon a shapeless shield of light. She wasn't as advanced as her mom, but it still worked.

"I WON'T LET YOU HURT THEM!" Kira roared, her speech becoming impossible to decipher as her mouth expanded and filled with razor sharp fangs.

Naomi was still staring into Knowledge's eyes, but she could see Kira transforming out of the corner of her eyes. She wanted to scream at her cousin to stop, but she was completely immobile.

Guru was quick to yank Eliza out of the way of a violent swipe of Kira's demonic claws. Enjay threw herself away from the attack's radius, ending up on Fate's opposite side, out of Naomi's field of vision.

With the group split up, Fate directed her attention to her biggest threat, Kira's demonic rage. Naomi, even out of her peripheral vision, was able to see the clear disgust in the immortal's face as she focused her attacks directly onto Kira. However, in her demonic state, Kira was much more agile than she could ever normally hope to be. She was able to slink back and forth with snakelike movements that crept up and allowed her a direct slash to Fate's nose, leaving a deep gash dripping with golden blood.

Fate screamed furiously, grabbing the demon before she was able to slink away, talon-like nails digging into her cousin's throat. The goddess dragged up the demon into the air and threw her across the cave. Naomi heard Guru's horrified scream as Kira crashed into the rock and cracked the stone around her from the impact.

Throughout all of the fighting, Naomi tried to wrench free of the invisible force holding her in place, but whatever Knowledge was doing to her was far more powerful than her own magic.

She couldn't escape.

Panic was circulating through her, making her body tingle uncomfortably. It took her a moment to realize that her body was trying to shake in fear as Fate loomed ever closer.

Enjay and Eliza had been knocked out of her range of vision. Guru was protecting an unconscious and bloody Kira from Fate's longer range attacks.

Fate was now standing in front of her. Her mouth opened in a hateful snarl. "You took my victory…" Fate began in a low voice, which got louder and more despicable with each word. "you took my **servant**, you took my **nemesis**, you took my **invention**! Now I'll take something from you."

Fate flicked her whip forcefully, the barbed coil capturing her arm and digging into Naomi's skin as it had so many years ago.

Naomi wanted to scream, to wail out in pain, but she couldn't even flinch. The agony rose up inside of her but couldn't escape.

"I think it's time I return the favor…" Fate gave Naomi a deranged smirk, her whip shrinking before the young woman's eyes.

Naomi stood, frozen and horrified as Fate began to slowly twist her whip, which was firmly anchored in the pink haired girl's arm.

Bile rose in Naomi's throat as she began to see the effects of the twisting. It was excruciating, white hot pain that throbbed unbearably, radiating from the site of impact to her shoulder, her shoulder popping from and crunching against its socket. She saw her skin and muscles snap out of the corner of her eye.

Fate was *ripping* her arm.

Just as the damage became irreversible and she heard the sickening and definite crack of bone, Knowledge closed his eyes and broke eye contact with Naomi.

She had control of her body again, but all she could do was cry out and sob until her vocal cords could no longer force out any noise.

She couldn't think, she couldn't hear anything over the hammering cacophony of her heart.

"I want to watch you bleed out and **die**, your life draining while you writhe helplessly in unyielding agony." Fate sneered, pulling her whip back.

Naomi's eyes widened in absolute terror. *No...*

"Say goodbye, ***Jack of Diamonds***." Fae whispered mockingly. She ripped away her whip,

Naomi could only scream and watch as the muscles of her arm ripped out of her body, dripping with horrifying rivers of blood.

Everything was red.

Sickeningly warm liquid was coating her side.

Naomi crashed to the floor, spotting Fate tossing the dislodged arm away as if it were a piece of trash. It landed next to Naomi with an unbearable squelching sound.

She couldn't take it. Seeing her mangled arm separate from the rest of her, feeling the blood run out of her stump of a shoulder; she threw herself to the side and heaved a considerable amount of acid and bile fleeing from her body.

There was a very muffled sound Naomi just barely picked up as her vision began to swim. Was that someone screaming? Why would they be... She couldn't even hold her thoughts long enough to finish the thought.

Her pain became duller. She could barely possess what was happening.

Naomi saw Fate's mouth moving.

Oh.

She was laughing. Laughing... at her? Why would Fate be laughing at her? Naomi could barely remember.

Naomi gasped, a sudden rush of clarity coming to her. Her arm, or what was left of it, throbbed horribly in her newfound consciousness.

The now bloody immortal moved towards the archway, which suddenly lit up in nebulous, purple light.

Fate paused, her head whipping to look at Knowledge, who was now holding what appeared to be a remote, in his pale hands. "W-what? But, *mon ange*, we are not ready-"

The god hummed, raising an angled brow. "Perhaps *you* are not, but **I am.**"

He pressed something that made the archway's light turn hazardous and bright. But despite that, Naomi saw her shadow nearing the archway, almost pulling away from her.

"No!" Fate completely focused on her male companion, completely ignoring the mortals she had been fighting. "We were supposed to do this together! I **LOVED** YOU-"

"I told you when we first met that I am not your ally, nor your lover; **we are business partners and nothing more.**"

"No..." Fate stepped back. Naomi was sure that she saw something inside the immortal snap. Fate was devastated, but the sorrow in her eyes clouded over much too quickly. She was in denial. "that can't be... because... you're my everything, so I must be yours!" She smiled brokenly, her eyes begging him for reciprocation desperately.

Knowledge was unmoved. "**No.**" He said, emotionless and insensitive as ever.

Naomi saw Fate's despair. For a split second, the immortal was overcome with betrayal, but... something shifted in her.

Fate was angry.

The goddess used her whip to steal the remote for the invention right out of Knowledge's hands. The male didn't even flinch.

Fate was breathing heavily, like she had been running. She ripped open the controls, grabbing a small, crystal orb out of a hidden compartment and holding it threateningly over her head.

"SAY IT AGAIN!" Fate yelled furiously.. "**I DARE YOU!** I'LL BREAK THIS AND RUIN **EVERYTHING** FOR YOU!"

Knowledge barely even rose a brow. "I regret nothing I said. I meant every word."

Fate let out a deranged wail as she threw the glass sphere to the stone ground with all her strength, tears of agony flowing down her face.

The nebulous substance residing in the archway began to swirl, quickly spreading up. Knowledge shook his head, his shoulders hunching up and down.

Is he... crying? Naomi couldn't tell.

Until he lifted his head, letting out a loud, bone-chilling laugh. There were tears in his eyes. For the first time since he had become immortal, every fiber of his being was filled with emotion.

Even Fate stared at him in shock, her pupils shrinking as she realized what she had done.

Knowledge gave Fate a gleeful smile. "Thank you, Fate."

The swirling became faster. As the portal sped up, a strange pull took hold of Naomi.

Her eyes widened as she watched her friends get sucked in and disappear one by one.

The last thing Naomi saw as she lost consciousness was Fate looking back at her, no longer looking sure of what she had do.

Piper Sehman is the author of the predecessor to the Naomi Serene Trilogy, Paradox, as well as the trilogy itself. She is currently attending Grand Canyon University for her bachelor's degree, but is always excited to visit her parents, brother and dog back home. Piper has undergone three brain surgeries, which have done nothing to dampen her passion for storytelling and writing, instead serving as motivation and inspiration for her work. Naomi Serene and The Quest for Knowledge is the second installment in its trilogy, building up the pre established world of Paradox while driving forward a plot with the stakes of not just our world, but reality itself hanging in the balance. Piper's mission is to continue to inspire others with her work and continue to explore and develop the worlds of her creation, encouraging them to live boldly and follow their dreams.